Memories, Light, & Promise

A Novel inspired by a true story of love.

Ramon Terrance Torry

Bloomington, IN  Milton Keynes, UK

AuthorHouse™
1663 Liberty Drive, Suite 200
Bloomington, IN 47403
www.authorhouse.com
Phone: 1-800-839-8640

AuthorHouse™ UK Ltd.
500 Avebury Boulevard
Central Milton Keynes, MK9 2BE
www.authorhouse.co.uk
Phone: 08001974150

© 2006 Ramon Terrance Torry. All rights reserved.

No part of this book may be reproduced, stored in a retrieval system, or transmitted by any means without the written permission of the author.

First published by AuthorHouse 8/3/2006

ISBN: 1-4259-3591-5 (sc)
ISBN: 1-4259-3590-7 (dj)

Printed in the United States of America
Bloomington, Indiana

This book is printed on acid-free paper.

This book is dedicated to my wife, Sherryl;
*My memories, my light,
and my promise.*

Embarkation

Every detective, investigator, profiler, and criminologist has a favorite case or those that stand out in their minds. What I am about to relay to you is the one case that will forever haunt my dreams. The hour is late into the night, it's very dark and I am depressed and sitting alone in my disheveled, little cubical. My fingers lick the key board, as I type up a report from my latest investigation. To be honest it's hard for me to concentrate, this is because even now I feel my mind drifting, swirling—no hurtling towards the events surrounding what I refer to as the "Episode."

The very rare few who know what happened have told me that the story would make a great movie, but being from Los Angeles, that always seemed too cliché. At times like this, late into the night, or early in the morning—depending upon your perspective—I have amused myself with the idea of writing it all down. In this I could deal with the torrential emotional and mental anguish I have suffered since that investigation. To be honest, my therapist recommended I write it out. I try but I hold back due to an ever nagging, and haunting of my own internal guilt. Even to this very night I remain suspicious of real motives for not putting this case behind me. I read once that with great power comes great responsibility that is on par with maturity. As I have gained greater maturity through the years I feel more responsible. I've learned that the more I mature, the more I am responsible and liable for my actions—and rightly so.

I've been through this emotional teeter-tottering before and I'm filled with resentment and excitement. "Shit, I hate doing this.... If my co-workers knew I had this material locked in my bottom drawer, they'd swear I was certifiable. I look at this information when I am alone in the office and the sun is in deep hiding from the moon. Every time I unlock and enter the recesses of my lower drawer and extract this case file, I feel foolish for even keeping it.

I now find myself entering Pandora's Box. The large manila folder packed with every scrap of evidence from the case.

I revisit it so much because somewhere in all the data I expect to find hope—not for myself, but for others. I stare at it like a cocaine addict going through withdrawals, and in need of a fix. I gape at the confines caught between its yellowish over stuffed maw that's being muzzled by a fat, thick red rubber band. I know it's my own self induced delirium, but the whole event takes on a life of its own, and I become nauseated and filled with loathing, understanding, and loss.

Try as I might, I attempt in futility to put the file away. As I fight with in my consciousness, I question why I'm so compelled to revisit this case I think I do so as self-punishment. Leafing through the personal letters, pictures, and holiday cards I shudder. I always pause when I get to the poems. I hate myself for trespassing here. It is at this point I take out something else that I shouldn't have in my drawer—whisky. It always takes a few shots of Jack Daniel's to help me get through the entire packet.

As time passes it's either Jack, my vivid imagination, or a combination of both, that transforms the events on these dead trees, from single dimensional script to three-dimensional images. It's as though I'm looking at a hologram of the events being played out in front of me, of course as I reach out, my hands pass through the images with little effort. This is the moment I decide to write the screenplay—a novel would be too involved and difficult. At first my thoughts race at computer-speed thinking; should I mask identities? Use aliases, and cloud the issues? However, if I do that I may lose something vital as I attempt to recreate the experience. I'm torn because someone may draw the correct conclusion and realize the truth. Then things would be difficult; the intricacies of the case would be exposed. Offensive attitudes, humiliating thoughts, and degrading opinions may spring forth causing pain. I imbibe more Jack and my thoughts slow, and I'm able to move on. One lingering thought remains though, "What is there to say, that a story like this one, would even make it to the silver screen?" This isn't a tale of gruesome, horrible, unspeakable acts of violence or of social deviancy; it isn't about political intrigue or espionage. The episode is a journey into something very tangible yet as elusive as will-o-the-wisp.

In all its manifestations commitment to another is as old-fashioned as Romeo and Juliet. These days love has been reduced to near-do-well television shows, or in the cinema, which has been placated and reduced to what I, in a condescending manner, call movie-love. Nonetheless, the case that keeps me in eternal turmoil is an account of love, true love, not something manufactured for celluloid, but something witnessed by me. The story is tragic, poignant, and extraordinary. I became involved in the case long before I realized it and each time I attempt to write the screenplay I feel like Judas, but instead of betraying Jesus, I feel I am betraying Heather, Heather Irving. My mixed emotions of loyalty are anesthetized as I swallow more of Mr. Daniels.

The screenplay software is already loaded on my PC—another office no-pas. It was long ago that I placed all the documents in chronological order, which makes the flow of my story easier to tell. I'm a pretty good investigator, if I do say so myself that and other insights make me confident that I can tell this tale. I gathered data at the site of the incident—which took place in the summer of '98, while an Army Reserve unit from Los Angeles, California, conducted its two week training—also known as Annual Training, AT for short.

I now sit like I use to on bill paying day—before I started paying them on line—with the documents spread before me. Extracts from Heather's diary, her letters, cards, poems, and a copy of the orders that sent the commander of the 69th Quartermaster Company, Major Thomas Michaels and Sergeant First Class Heather Irving to Camp Pendleton, California, all lay open, ready to once again be violated by me. I also have the sworn statements of the unit's platoon leaders, first sergeant, and other officers and non-commissioned officers, and inquiries conducted by myself.

I often romanticize about Thomas Michaels. I can ad-lib certain things about him because I found myself obsessed to find out all I could about the man. After a thorough investigation, I resented the fact that there wasn't anything bizarre. He was a likable and down-to-earth person. I could see myself hanging out with him, throwing back a few beers, watching a football or hockey game. As an officer his record was impeccable! The men and women in his unit loved him. He was professional, by the book, and a natural leader. That was another puzzling aspect that was contradictory of the behavior he displayed during that two weeks. Heather refers to him in her diary as a man's man, endowed with the innate ability to identify with a woman's needs on mental-emotional, spiritual and physical levels. People closest to him said he fancied himself a person set out of season, as though he didn't belong in the summer, winter, spring, or autumn. Some of his poems, which I have in the file, allude to this. When he wasn't playing Army on the weekends, he held a full time job as an artist for an ad agency. I unearthed a few drawings he had done for major advertisers and a few personal ones—they were well done. After the episode he was stripped of his rank and drummed out of the Army, but I still remained intrigued and followed his trail. I knew bringing Heather, Heather Irving to life would not be as difficult as Major Michaels, she expressed herself well through her writing, but left a wealth of work behind in her diary that was chock full of tidbits into her psyche.

It often happens this way; I get it all set in my mind and like most screenplays the first-line reads: FADE IN, that's when I pause, absorb a mouthful of Jack and pray. You see, I have become rather jaded. I was married once and I've investigated, read, or observed hundreds of cases involving relationships until my attitude became very cynical even though I was unaware of it. It's after being educated—for a lack of a better word—by this case, that I have realized what is attainable from the true alliance of one heart to another. I wish that it hadn't taken MAJ Michaels, and Heather, Heather Irving to instruct me in the ways of love. All things considered, I have learned that relationships can be as great as any play scripted by Shakespeare, or any book written by romance novelists that dare to show the true meaning of amour. That is another reason I want to get this screenplay out, because just maybe someone else may see or read this and understand—maybe.

Being a man, what I want to write makes this difficult for me. Even harder is convincing anyone of the authenticity of the episode.

Like most individuals on the planet, I harbored my own self-fulfilling ideologies of right, wrong, decency, and what is and isn't sensible, when it comes to matters of adulation, passion, and love. Before the episode, I was insensitive and unsympathetic. Books, movies, plays, and even television always dripped with over-sentimentality, and I have a propensity to mock and hold true love in contempt.

Therefore, it makes it near impossible to make the shift over to a different season. The shift was very hard because the episode involving MAJ Michaels and Heather, Heather Irving asked me to forget that I was an Army Officer, myself and back then I was still married.

As I sit in front of my computer with Jack and my notes and all the paper work next to the keyboard, I deduce through an ever growing haze that all my trepidation means nothing if the screenplay isn't written, sold and produced, well-cast and directed, and on the big screen. Even if all this happened and I colored it with purple-prose I wonder if anyone will experience what I did during that time and the intensity of that brief moment at the end. That's when I take yet another swallow and hunker down over the keyboard.

So I ask you to imagine yourself entering the theater or reading in a nice quiet spot. Leave everything you think you know about love outside or in the other room as you engulf the sights and sounds stirring in your own imagination. Remember, this is a true story told to you on good, honest and reliable authority. I am convinced that when you read THE END and/or see the credits roll, or close the book you will know that MAJ Michaels and Heather, Heather Irving did reside in a different season that One Annual Training.

Memories,
Light, &
Promise.
A Novel inspired by a true story of love

Love bears all things, believes all things, hopes all things, and endures all things. Love never fails.
                        1 Corinthians 13:7-8

1
Major Thomas Michaels

At twilight, on the first day the Main Body was to leave for Annual Training, Thomas Michaels had just finished the latest sketches for the print-ad he worked on all week. He would be gone for two weeks and didn't want to miss the deadline a week away.

He compressed the work into a .jpg file, brought up his e-mail, attached the data, and forwarded it to McMillan, Hartford & Ryan. Within the hour he had showered, and donned his woodland-green camouflaged Battle Dress Uniform (BDU). After dropping a 14-day feeder into the fish tank, he retrieved his laptop computer and secured the door of his two-bedroom, contemporary-furnished condominium. He was one of the lucky ones, his condo was on the corner-end and his garage was attached.

After activating the automatic garage door, he popped the rear of his late model black Ford Explorer. Thomas checked the back bed of the Sport Utility Vehicle and ensured his duffel bag, back-pack, and footlocker was all in place. They were where he left them seven hours earlier. He closed the back door and mumbled something about how Ford should put pneumatic pressure on the door. As he sat in the front seat, he laid the laptop on his portfolio and a few loose sketches. He started the engine and backed the truck out into the awaking morning.

The digital clock on the dashboard read 5:45 AM. It was still too early to get an oat-bran muffin and a Venti Café Americano from Starbucks.

As Thomas traveled down Ocean Boulevard, he glanced toward the sunrise. The burgeoning daystar's light against the horizon of the Pacific Ocean was a glorious sight. He turned left onto Santa Monica Boulevard, knowing he would soon be locked in the woods with 130 soldiers conducting training and maneuvers', preparing young men and women to fight to keep American's free to observe such sights. He took pride in being the company commander of his unit; it filled him with a certain amount of satisfaction to know he had a minute-hand in keeping democracy alive. He loved America, despite all her shortcomings, and on some rudimentary level he was never ashamed to say it.

Approaching the 405 North, his stomach growled.

"Hey, I'll put something in you soon," he said aloud to himself.

Being a bachelor, Thomas never found the time to keep his refrigerator stocked, or the will to prepare meals in the morning. The ladies that vied for his attention fed him well, and someone brought doughnuts to the office on a regular basis. He thought about those doughnuts as he pulled onto the freeway.

Thomas Michaels didn't mind being single; he had come close to marriage once, but never arrived at the altar. He was born a twin. He and his sister, Tonya, did everything together. They were close - amalgamated to one another until her final breath.

Tonya died at six years of age.

Riding her bike, during one of their childish games of chase, she lost control and fell. Her head hit the concrete and cracked her skull—leaving Thomas the only child.

Thomas kept Tonya's gold-chained keepsake, a half-hearted necklace, to which he had the other half. It was a present for their fifth birthday. Inscribed on it was "When together, we are one." He wore both of them everyday following that terrible incident. Thomas' parents overprotected him, and showered him with a weighted affection—a possible paranoia. The guilt of Tonya's loss may have anchored them to never bring another child into the world. When he was seventeen, his parents were killed in an automobile accident. He never pursued any of his relatives, and had no clues where they might be. He socialized at a minimum with the people at the office and the troops of the unit. His relationships with his civilian and military bosses were official and reserved.

When he passed the Getty Center exit, Thomas was reminded of Johanna Getty, a talented and attractive woman he had fallen in love with. She was there for him through his parent's passing. He asked her to marry him when they graduated from high school. They were both 18 and she was more practical than he was. She had been accepted to Julliard in New York, and he had a scholarship to University California-Los Angeles (UCLA). She told him she would consider his proposal after she finished college.

They entered the long-distance relationship thing, and like so many others they never considered its initial doom. And like a mission to Mars, distance and time were unforgiving. Thomas would visit and be with some of Johanna's new friends and feel like a fifth wheel. Despite frequent visits, telephone calls and letters, they drifted apart. Two years later, Johanna called and informed Thomas she was leaving school because she was pregnant by her instructor. He never let her hear him cry. She asked him to forgive her and he did.

"If things don't work out with your instructor, I would love to take care of you and the child," he told her.

Though she promised they would always remain close, Johanna's guilt and shame kept her from honoring the vow. Many months passed and Thomas hadn't received a response to any of his letters. They began coming back, RETURN TO SENDER, and then he knew it was time for him to let go.

At Burbank Boulevard he headed toward the Army Reserve Center. The center was like his second home. In the 18 months he had been in command, he had spent at least 40 hours a week conducting military business. The brick exterior gave off a staunch, cold air about the place, while the yellowish puke-colored walls and fluorescent-lighted interior made it seem downright uninviting. His unit took up space on the first floor and another unit resided upstairs.

As Major Michaels entered the parking lot he found several troops camped out in their cars waiting. He was the first to arrive with a key to the building and knew that the kids in their cars had been frightened by their platoon sergeants not to miss movement. He thought he'd open the center and then go to the Starbucks on the corner. It would be safe for him at this hour—Annette wasn't there yet. She was the store manager, 38, and attractive. They went out on dates at times. She was divorced, no kids and easy-going. Their relationship was supposed to be plutonic. However, after a few movies, dinners and free coffee they found themselves in bed. The sex was great and she fell for him, but for him the feelings weren't mutual. He had to break it off because he didn't want to give her false hopes. The day it ended, he could hear the misery in her voice as they quarreled. During this time of intense emotional stress, she was endowed with the clairvoyance that comes when one speaks from true fervor. Her parting words chilled him deep inside.

"You don't love me. I pity you. You touch, feel, and empathize with warmth, but a huge part of you is cold and distant."

Long ago, Thomas learned from the women he dated, and those yet to come, a consistent assessment evolved from their frustrations with him. Each of the women seemed resolved in the idea of having him as a life partner. However, he discounted their efforts which caused them to feel contempt for their own value, and he learned no woman wanted to feel as though she were worthless.

This was not psycho-babble. In an uncanny way, Annette hit on something in Thomas which was more fact than fiction. He didn't clearly remember everything about his sister, but since her death he had been able to channel a tangible sense of her spirit. This unconscious conduit let him drift on a riff in time that gave him creative and emotional power that defied what was consciously possible. From time to time he would draw or write a poem that was plain, but constructed with elements that had intricate, complex and deep meaning. One such poem was:

Mythology of Love

The mythology of love is simple, made complex by nature and humans
It's whimsical, placid, and enigmatic when defined or honed
Scientists and scholars discuss, the embodiment
of pheromones or endorphins
Others, lie, cheat and tease for they've discovered evidence in its trends
Popular thought leans towards a connection
with friendship that has grown

Laws of religion and man are intricacies conceded
to pleasures unaware as we try to quell great desires
Others circumspect journey for amorous' offerings of their soul for blood
Marriage vows malign and exalt; still we mum something basic of its creed
And weathering pains to extinguish its wild fires

Out cry protects us as we commit moral criminalities
The intangible pondered; soul-mates, destiny, credit chance
Insecure we become selfish organisms in slime
A need perpetrated like myths and false-Gods, sustained by belief and time
Love's satisfaction covers a range of nouns and ambiguous dance

The mythology of love is simple, made complex by nature and humans
It's whimsical, placid, and even enigmatic when defined or honed
Scientists and scholars discuss the embodiment
of pheromones or endorphins
Others, lie, some cheat and tease for they discovered evidence in its trends
The truth be told, love is mythologized to
safeguard our fear of being alone.

Thomas let these things pass over him as he opened the door to his small comfortable office. There was a desk, computer table, a small, cherry wood bookcase, and a medium-sized conference table. Opposite each other in the two front corners sat the American flag on the left and the California state flag on the right. The right wall contained a window. To the left were his certificates, diplomas, and awards. He never liked 'posturing' his credentials and achievements, but to disobey a direct-order by the battalion commander could prove more problematic than eccentricity.

"I've seen your records, said Lieutenant Colonel Baker. "You're an intelligent young man and I'd be remiss if I didn't have you display your credentials."

"Sir, with all due respect, he replied. "I don't need an ego wall to let anyone know what my abilities are. Transcripts, awards, and letters of commendation are a poor way to measure a person."

LTC Baker raised an eyebrow, and said, "In this command it's by my order that all company commanders display their awards and certificates."

Thomas followed orders.

All his life, Thomas was an outstanding student on both the civilian- and military-side of the house. He had received a full-academic scholarship to University of Southern California (USC) and was approached for the football and track teams. He was built solid, and endowed with the muscularity and symmetry of a sprinter. However, he had no real desire for sports, but did like adventure and discovery. For that reason, he joined the Reserve Officer Training Corps (ROTC) on campus. He distinguished himself as a leader. He had a good mind and strong, soft hands. Expressionist art was his pastime - the Warrior Artist, they called him at school.

After graduating, he spent several years on active duty in the military. He went in as an Intelligence officer, but after years of planning and participating in covert operations, he transferred to the logistics branch. He found more time to sketch, illustrate, paint, and create. His passion for the craft burned anew and when he made the rank of captain he knew it was time for him to get out of the full-time military. That was seven years ago.

He worked hard at perfecting his talent and returned to school to study graphic and computer art. It was during this time he was introduced to the world of commercial art. He found this was a perfect way to express his creativity and skill. The job paid well and allowed him to travel. He began as an assistant and then after two years was hired as the Art director for McMillan, Hartford & Ryan. He ran the art department as he did his command: efficient. Most thought this was because of his military background, but he knew it was more than that. There was talk in the company that within five years, he would become partner. Thomas never paid much attention to the talk and focused to do his best.

None of these things were on his mind today. He had an itch to get some coffee and something to eat. As fate would have it, he wasn't in his office ten minutes before the First Sergeant (1SG) Hillman came in bearing doughnuts. The First Sergeant was a big black man with curled hair and a moon face. He was a mechanical engineer in his civilian profession.

"The advance party loaded everything yesterday, sir. I have a few men to help load the weapons," Hillman said.

"Good, good." Major Thomas replied in between gulps of coffee.

"Oh, and by the way, we have two new troops joining us for this Annual Training."

"I'll give them the new comer's spiel when we get to the field." Thomas responded.

"Hooah sir! I'll come and get you when the main body is ready to move out."

"Hooah!" Thomas replied.

It took two hours for Hillman to have the company formed and the convoy ready to roll, and it was then that Thomas found himself sitting on the passenger side of his HUMVEE staring at the training schedules, duty roster's, and the personnel list.

As they made the transition from the 405 to 5 freeways he looked behind and saw the six convoys still maintaining their proper intervals. He then turned his attention back to the roster. His eyes searched columns and rows of the excel spreadsheet, then halted when he came to her name. He was momentarily mystified.

He met the two new troops before the formation and said no more than hello to them when the unit clerk introduced them and explained she had processed them in during the week. Nonetheless, of the two soldiers, both were female. One of them had stirred something in him; something from a level of consciousness he was surprised existed. He didn't think of how attractive she was, although she was—he somehow perceived her attractiveness was from within. It was perplexing to him and try as he might, he couldn't escape the strange familiarity about her. He warned himself to be on guard and for the first time since he took command, he didn't want to give the new comer's brief. And it had something to do with the new soldier, because what he sensed had agitated his soul.

2
Sergeant First Class Heather, Heather Irving

It's a phenomenon that happens twice a year. An equinox. It's when the sun crosses the equator and day and night everywhere are of equal length. This September Heather actually *feels* herself within the great circle of the celestial sphere. At the point where the celestial equator intersects the ecliptic is where she watches. It's here that she escapes her past and looks to her future. She was nude under a silk robe in the backyard. Her body reclined on one of the lawn chairs feeling, waiting, thinking—as the night winds caressed her body, kissing her legs, waist, nipples, and lips. The silk robe was no more than an excuse at dignity. If anyone were to find her and see her reddish-brown locks whipping in the wind, her knees bent, and spread-wide, they'd think she was more than eccentric, perhaps intoxicated—they would be wrong with both assumptions.

Bruce was far from her thoughts. They had been divorced for two years. Irreconcilable differences seemed as good a term as any to sum up the 40 plus years of marriage. And with their child Toby through college, med school, residence, and marriage the tide of responsibility had ebbed. Bruce was a military man: strong, benign, and consistent. Those qualities proved great for the army, but not as her husband.

In the settlement she got the house in Thousand Oaks where she now resided alone. Of course, friends would escape the slow drumbeat of their lives and they would come together like studio musicians and play the background that gave her voice rhythm. They'd converse and reminisce about their lives, gossip about their children, and remark on things they had no real clue about. She didn't mind and on occasion enjoyed their company. But she never told them anything too personal. They wouldn't comprehend. It wasn't that she was different from them; *she was just different from them.* The difference was internal, somewhere on a plane of being that didn't hold with every popular belief about life, people, and love.

Bruce had always told her, "You're like a chameleon; you have the ability to blend in with your environment. That's the only reason why I can see you having those women for friends."

What Bruce didn't realize was that ability aided her in blending with him. She did care about him. In his own way he was a very wonderful man. They had met in college, University of Southern California. He played football and she was a calculus tutor. When she began tutoring him, the only definition of limit he knew was something that bounds, restrains, or confines. However, by the time she was through, he understood in simple mathematical terms, it is the intended height of a function. Limits were the value, as x approaches a number, and didn't have to reach that number. Meaning that there could be a hole or a removable discontinuity at the x value, but as x gets closer to that number y is also growing closer to a number and that number is your limit.

Though attractive, she was brainy. Most of the guys that were in her league were too conservative, and the ones that were handsome didn't have the gray matter to keep her interest. Bruce, with his rugged good looks and brain that wanted to be great, made her realize that maybe her standards were too high, and the superman she was looking for didn't exist. Aside from playing football, Bruce was in the ROTC, and did seem destined to make something of himself. After suffering an injury that kept him from playing football, but not severe enough to keep him from getting his commission as an officer, he asked her to marry him—unknowing that she was carrying his child. She kept the news from him hoping that he'd ask. She didn't want to feel she had trapped him, and have him stay out of guilt. Being an only child, she was independent, and had figured if Bruce didn't ask, she would raise the child herself. Nonetheless, she was pleased when he did.

The California air—despite all the talk of smog—made her think better. The Santa Anna winds cleansed the night atmosphere with a gust from its nostrils, leaving the sky fresh and alive with scents of the sea and poppies. The air bath was as close as she could come to remembering Thomas's touch. It was like this during both equinox's March and September. It was a lone sheet of paper that gave way to sanity—-protected within a plastic transparent document pouch was the 8 x 11 sheet safe from the circling breeze. Eyes shut, mind racing, Heather wasn't crazy or drunk. She was remembering the greatest love of her life. Like the warm flow of air across her breasts, she could feel his hands, like the gentle current between her thighs she could feel his breath. In her hand was the poem, the catalyst to their beginning and their end. It was handwritten in black India ink. The script was calligraphy from pens artists' use. It was a poem that touched her and despite its ominous, overtones did indeed speak to her heart and made her **Bite the Apple**.

As she laid there in a naked bliss within the far reaches of her mind, she was reliving every detail of her time with Thomas—and that fateful Annual Training so many years ago. Since dwelling in that different season with him, she worked hard at putting the pieces together and tried to understand what happened. He had put it so succinctly once in his tent.

He looked deep into her eyes, and said, "You may not understand this, but you are my limit."

She went weak in the knees. She understood it better than he knew. However, when her tears fell, he understood before she responded.

"These last few days you have made me happy because, as my feelings are x and getting closer to that intangible thing called love, like y, I'm growing closer to a number, and that number is you—my limit."

Her thoughts were powerful and vivid. He had never been to this house, but it felt as though he was beside her. The images produced in her mind made Technicolor look matted. She could see Thomas standing tall at six feet, two inches, broad shoulders, and an athletic physique. He was in his camouflage, and as his steel blue eyes peeked out from his matching cap, she felt him touch her soul. They were introduced, and he said, "Hello." That moment was electric, and she sensed he felt the charge, too. As he stood erect in front of the formation she had to check herself to ensure no one noticed her gushing. She was embarrassed and afraid. This was her first drill with this unit and she was going to spend two weeks with people she didn't know, and she already felt something for the commander. This was strange. Handsome men didn't turn her on. She never fantasized about strangers, and in all her 34 years. Never had anyone captivated her with a simple 'hello'. Her nipples were erect and she felt moisture where there shouldn't have been any. This never happened around Bruce, even when they had been in the flowery stages of courtship.

The wind gusted harder and Heather moved.

"Thomas?" she murmured, as if from a dream.

It wasn't until later that she knew he loved her. It wasn't in his compliments it was his look around the campsite. He would stop and stare at her, and even with her back turned, she could sense the warmth of his gaze as he engulfed every detail of her: hazel eyes, pout lips, and disheveled fiery hair. He had caught a glimpse of her coming from the field showers and was able to capture her lean muscularity and toned skin to its exact peach-pink hue. His ability with the pen and colored pencils was extraordinary. She remembered thinking she had never looked that good. She was never one for self-admiration, despite all the compliments and sexual offers she received from men and women. But it was that Annual Training her mind drifted back to as the wind settled once more. She had watched Major Thomas secretly as she dragged her gear into the women's tent, trying to understand the mental, emotional, and physical confusion he had put her in.

"Move it, troop!" a voice boomed from the back.

Inside the tent she noticed the advance party personnel had set up cots in neat little rows. As she laid her duffel bag down a female whispered to her.

"I saw ya looking at the Major. Let me tell you, forget about it. The girls think he's gay."

She took that as a compliment to him. On some strange level she knew he wasn't. *He just wasn't interested in them.* Heather thought. Aloud she asked, "Why would you say that?"

"Well he's tall, about 40, unmarried, handsome, and we never see him with any girls." A blonde female soldier remarked.

"Yeah, I flirted with him and didn't get so much as an eye batted in my direction," a pretty girl with a southern accent replied.

It was two hours later after this conversation that Heather and Private First Class (PFC) Marie Norby found themselves in the tent designated as the orderly room being briefed by Major Thomas and First Sergeant Hillman. They all sat in small metal field chairs. Heather tried not to show her embarrassment, as Thomas seemed to focus his attention on her as he spoke. She was pleased but concerned that PFC Norby and 1SG Hillman would notice his stares.

As the meeting went on, she found herself caring less and less if the other two noticed or what they might be thinking. As they sat going over the mission of the unit, the organizational table, and how each platoon fit to make up the company, she was watching his lips. She was warmed at the thought of his mouth on hers, and his lips tenderly placing kisses all over her body. Never had she fantasized about Bruce in this way and became aware in that instant she needed to leave the tent.

"Excuse me, sir, may I step outside a moment I need a bit of air," Heather exclaimed calmly.

Without saying a word, Major Thomas nodded his head and pointed to the open flap of the tent.

Heather left without reservation.

She must have been outside longer than she expected, because, it wasn't until Norby, Hillman and Thomas exited the tent that she realized fifteen minutes had passed.

"Are you okay Sergeant Irving?" Hillman questioned.

"Yes, First Sergeant, I don't know what came over me in there. All of a sudden, it felt as though the air was choking me."

Its okay, it's balmy out here and those old tents do get pretty stuffy. Especially out here in the woods."

We were about finished anyway." Thomas added. "There are a couple of items I need to go over and we can cover those out here. I won't make you go back into the tent."

"Thank you, Sir."

"If you got this Major I'll take PFC Norby over to the mess tent it's about time for chow."

"Roger. We'll follow directly, Top." Thomas replied.

Within a few moments they were alone. She never felt so nervous in all her life. Within the past fifteen minuets, she had convinced herself that she was being irrational, immature, and stupid. As she stood she felt beads of perspiration descend from her armpits. For the first time she became aware that she was outside and didn't have her headgear on. In an instant her thoughts went to her hair. Though up in a military bun and held tight by a few dozen bobby pins she thought maybe her red locks were touching her collar. She took a breath and looked up at Major Thomas. Before their eyes met, she covered the four inches that separated them in height by looking at his starched uniform, endowed with Airborne and Air assault wings. She noticed the chain of his dog tags, glinting out from his brown tee shirt, as the top button of his shirt was undone and the collar laid flat against his chest. Her gaze took her up and across his wide shoulders, stout neck, protruding Adams apple, square chin and back to his lips."

Are you sure you're okay?" Thomas asked as their eyes met. His tone was familiar, comfortable, and concerned, as though he'd asked this question before, on many occasions to her, during a lifetime of being together.

And just as familiar and comfortable she replied. "Oh, it's nothing, I'll be all right."

Thomas smiled baring straight white healthy teeth, thanks to two years of braces, and two years of a retainer. "I bet you will at that." His words surprised him but he didn't comment further.

The moment their eyes met, and as Thomas looked at her, she felt something stirring inside. Then the way he spoke, his voice it was as if he'd done this before. It was something in his steel blue eyes, taught facial muscles, twitch of his brow, familiar—disturbing, comfortable. She knew this man, she didn't know how but, she knew him and sensed he knew her, but this was crazy, she had never seen him or heard his voice before today. If she weren't awake, she'd swear she was dreaming a recurring dream. One in which this character was a part of her, and had been for a long time. *"They say everyone has a soul mate - a person perfectly matched one for the other. Could this be hers?"* The thought lingered. She sensed a kinship. This was happening too fast, but, then again where is it written these things should take time, and who says it doesn't happen like this, she felt something between them pulling at them on a sub-molecular level. It was as if her being possessed a property, attracting his life force, and producing a magnetic-like field, external to themselves. There was an extraordinary powerful force at work and she felt it.

A soldier half out of breath came running up, "Excuse me sir, Mess Sergeant wants you. Say's its important. It's about the chow, might not be enough."

"Tell Sergeant Heller, I'll be right there." Thomas responded. Then he turned to Heather. After being in the active and reserve army for over fifteen years, very well versed in the rules and regulations governing fraternization, and the protocol between officers and enlisted soldiers Thomas was in complete consternation when he said, "Come with me. I'll see what the problem is and we can talk over lunch. That's if you want too?"

What did he say that for, he wasn't even sure it was him speaking? It felt like he was a compass and she was his magnetic north. He found himself not wanting to stray from her direction.

He sensed that she was surprised by his offer, not so much that he offered, but that he said it. Whatever was happening between them, he knew that this was a military setting, he was her commanding officer, and she was married. He deduced that somehow, either she, or he, or they, had drawn each other near on some intangible level after moments of close proximity.

"That would be nice." She said without hesitation.

Thomas rejoiced and cursed to himself at her answer. He knew he wasn't strong enough to divert the pull she had engulfed him in, and in the back of his mind he was hoping she would be the strong one and halt this before it went any farther.

"Then let's go. They turned and hurried off towards the mess tent.

Thomas passed the soldiers going through the chow line. As the commanding officer he knew he would eat last and if there wasn't enough food for his soldiers he wouldn't eat at all.

Twenty minutes had passed since she saw him enter the mess tent, time enough for her to go through the chow line, be seated, and eat half of her lunch. There wasn't much too it just over cooked mixed vegetables, spaghetti noodles with meat sauce, chicken, a salad which was all iceberg lettuce and a piece of pound cake covered with vanilla frosting. Heather new she hadn't joined the army for its cuisine, and this was better than the prepackaged, dehydrated food that would become the mainstay of their noon diet. She was startled as a voice caught her by surprise, "Eat up, it could be an MRE." The voice said jokingly. Heather cocked her head and with a quick movement of her eyes she starred at a dirty blonde female approaching her position. As she recognized PFC Norby she smiled and replied. "I know what you mean, those Meals Ready to Eat make me want to hurl."

From the opposite direction she was in total consternation as Thomas seemed to magically appear. "Well, get used to it, for the next few days that's all we'll be eating."

Both of the women's faces dropped.

"It seems the mess sergeant didn't draw enough A-rations for lunch and dinner meals for the whole two weeks, so he'll have to stretch it a bit. I think it's better during the first week as opposed to the later half. " Thomas added.

Heather watched him as he set his tray down on the weather damaged wooden picnic table, and then took a seat a meter from her. There was a fluid like flow to his movements a kin to water flowing over rock in a creek bed—constant, unrestrained, and easy. He looked at her, his eyes never glancing away as he spoke; the expression on his face was mixed with disturbed curiosity.

In contrast to what was on her and PFC Norby's tray he had fruit, two red apples, two oranges and a cup of water. She glanced at his bare forearms as they jutted out from the rolled up sleeves of his uniform. They looked toned, and she could tell the rest of his body matched. The sun was deepening the tan on his arms and seemingly to apply its rays evenly.

Memories, Light, & Promise

"Don't worry Sir; we can handle the dehydrated stuff." PFC Norby said condescendingly.

With PFC Norby around Thomas began to feel a bit flustered, and now a little ashamed at his initial feelings towards Heather. As Thomas sat, he still felt the arguable pangs of attraction and the resistance of their separation. He quickly sized upon a topic that would distract if not fully release his growing desire of this women.

"So Sergeant Irving how is it that you've come to join the fighting 69th?"

Heather still had spaghetti in her mouth. She motioned with her hands as she finished chewing and swallowing. With a smile that seemed to mock the one painted by Da-Vinci on the Monalisa she said, "Actually sir, I was promoted into your unit. I initially joined the Reserves to give me something to do. And since my husband was already in the Reserve, it wasn't too hard for me to get in.

"Husband a recruiter?" Thomas asked.

No. Nothing like that. Actually he's an officer, and I don't think you know him unless you get into some kind of trouble, and even then you probably won't know who he is."

As she spoke she knew she wasn't offending him. In the back of her mind she kept thinking—there is something about him. Something not quite average, something awfully familiar, it was in his look, his voice, his manner. She locked eyes with him at the end of her sentence. And immediately stole a glimpse into his soul. Later she would know it was more of a glimmer, a dim perception or idea she saw when their eyes fixed firmly. What she saw looking back in that fleeting moment, was her heart.

And though speaking in general she caught herself in total surprise when she said. "I always knew I'd come and join you,"—the words hung in the air like a humming bird, just long enough for you to see him but never long enough to see his wings. And before any comment was rendered Heather finished, "Yeah, once I enlisted I always knew I'd get promoted and join other units. I knew about this unit and the opening when my paper work for promotion went up."

Noticing a spot of tomato sauce in the corner of her mouth, Thomas instinctively handed her a napkin. The movement seemed customary, yet it concealed a personal intimacy in the act. As she took the napkin her right index finger touched his every so slightly, but in that moment, it was long enough to feel the tenderness of his touch and heat of his flesh."

And as she wiped her mouth he said, "I'm glad you've come." The statement was simple in its reply, but profound all the same.

For the next ten minutes there was silence as everyone finished chow. Heather, mother of one and wife to a military officer finished second. She didn't get right up, she sat for a moment or two as her food began to digest. Thomas had finished his apples and oranges, smiled warmly in her direction and excused himself seconds earlier. She now watched as he carried his bare tray save the husk of his oranges and the empty Styrofoam cup that held his water, back to the mess tent. From the back she could tell his body was hard, devoid of the excess lipids that seem to have invaded and then took over Bruce's body. It wasn't that Bruce was overly corpulent and Thomas emaciated, she just could see the difference between what a balanced diet, coupled with exercise, had done for Thomas and one full of doughnuts, McDonald's, and pizza had done for Bruce. In the recesses of her mind she knew it wasn't all Bruce's fault—part of his diet was a reflection of his job.

It was nice, at least right here right now. She saw a field mouse scurry into a hole, dragging a hunk of bread that some how missed the trash. A few crows were crowing as though to be upset that they didn't get the bread. The warmth of the yellow summer sun was just the remedy that made the breeze perfect to enjoy.

As Thomas closed in on the mess tent he was approached by several troops. He stood for a moment, answered questions, and pointed in the direction of a dry streambed as if to indicate training taking place over there.

Heather picked up her tray and along with PFC Norby, rose and headed for the trash bins. She noticed several of the guys looking in their direction—checking them out. Norby noticed them to, "It must be the heat girl that makes men pant so." she remarked.

"Yeah," Heather acknowledged, 'You would think the breeze would cool them off." The two girls laughed simultaneously.

Heather no longer saw Thomas, and subconsciously her eyes were searching the camp ground for him. When she did locate him, due to the position of the sun, she could see his arresting silhouette down by the dry stream bed.

He was walking with the First Sergeant, and they must have been on a decline because as they moved she saw his legs, waist, shoulders and head disappear in that order.

As she dumped the debris of her lunch into the trash she could hear the voices of the soldiers and one of the platoon leaders barking out commands to hurry and finish chow. There would be a formation in five minuets. An hour or so had passed before she saw Thomas again, and though her thoughts never left him, she was surprised by his return. "So how are they treating you?" He had asked as he tapped her on the shoulder.

She knew the voice without seeing him. She knew it as well as her own. What she hadn't realized was that it was so close—right up on her. "Sir." she echoed and turned. Her pupils dilated. As the astonishment diminished, they returned to normal.

"I found this along the creek bed." He said this as he handed her a piece of quartz crystal. The object was near transparent and colorless.

The instant she took it from his hand she shuddered. For a brief instant the quartz seemed to come alive. The electric field of energy surrounding their bodies oscillated, and adjusted as it seemed to set a constant frequency for them – *to regulate them.*

Thomas felt the supernatural tug, and noticed Heather did as well. He dismissed it immediately and smiled as he asked, "You okay?"

"I don't know." She said, something strange just happened, but I'm fine now." She looked at the crystal and thought, *"Was it this? Naw! Probably the final part of my lunch digesting or something."*

"I just wanted to say thanks for sharing your time with me at lunch. And when I saw that," Thomas pointed at the quartz in her hand, "I thought it was pretty and I thought of you."

"Thank you." She replied trying not to blush. Before another word was spoken Thomas was being pulled away by the First Sergeant on yet another matter.

Heather stretched her hand wide—palm up and balanced the piece of crystal. Rays of the sun were peeking out from the clouds; one such ray caught the quartz. As she gazed at the crystal, now brilliantly clear, she drifted; a psychic state of divination was induced. She felt

Thomas Michaels, on a plain of existence that she could not discern or comprehend. All she knew was that she wanted—no needed to know more about him. As her hand closed tightly on the crystal, she could feel her heart rate increase as her blood was being pumped faster, igniting her from within. Instinctively she dropped the crystal, as though it was the cause of her plight. She felt ashamed and embarrassed. A wave of guilt washed over her. Heather bent to pick up the crystal subconsciously soothing her soul, *"You have done nothing wrong, you haven't said anything, or done anything, you have not offended Bruce."*

As she picked up the quartz, she felt better; taking one last look at it she smiled and tucked it safely in the left pocket of her BDU.

"What are you doing standing there?" A friendly voice questioned

Heather turned to see it was PFC Norby. She was waving her over to some camouflaged netting. Heather moved in her direction.

"We new girls gotta stick together," Norby said. "I figure me and you can be partners putting-up this cammo-netting. If you want."

"Sure", Heather said as she grabbed a bag of poles.

"You seem kind of quiet. You all right?" Norby questioned.

"I'm fine." Heather said evenly. "How about yourself?"

"Me!?" Norby answered in surprised. "I'm okay." She picked up a pack of netting. "Top wants us to do the commanders tent. It's small and Major Michaels will actually help us."

Within thirty minutes the two soldiers were at the commanders' tent. Thomas stepped out of his tent just as they arrived with the netting and poles.

"So it's you two again?" He questioned playfully.

"Yes sir. Top assigned us to help you." Norby said.

"Well then let's get to work."

They worked diligently and quickly. It took them twenty minuets to lay out the poles, sew the netting and drape it over the tent. Heather tried desperately not to stare or ask too many questions, but she couldn't help noticing his strong back and wide shoulders as he worked. She also tried to ignore the fact that he was watching her. He took off his cap, and wiped at the perspiration on his forehead.

"It's getting hot." Thomas exclaimed. "Why don't we take a water break?" They all reached for their canteens.

"Damn it! I never filled mine up." Norby said sounding disappointed.

"I'd give you some of mine but its best you fill yours up at the water buffalo." Heather instructed.

"Make sure you use the one that says potable water." Thomas added.

"Yes Sir", Norby said as she carried her empty canteen over to the area that held the drinking water.

Heather watched Thomas take a long sip from his canteen.

Thomas in turn watched Heather as she took a small drink. She was very pretty, middle-thirty's, and stood about five feet-seven inches. He could tell even in her uniform that she exercised regularly. But as he watched her he still found his attraction for her puzzling. Yes she was pretty, but he had known lots of beautiful women. Each time he was in her presence he had yet to fully realize, that it was her interior beauty that drew him, as opposed to her eye-pleasing exterior. Total awareness of her began to dawn after he gave her the crystal. It was as though it was a catalyst that magnified and had somehow given him clearer insight into a certain percentage of her spirit entity. He couldn't explain it and didn't dare try. He thought—*no knew*, he knew her, resided with her, if not physically, then spiritually. He knew her intelligence, knew her sensuality, knew her passion and knew her soul. It was a bond he felt a very long time ago, when he was very young and his sister was alive. Heather, somehow possessed or had the ability to open his eyes and give him sight. Not through his organ of sight but through eyes of his mind, spirit, and inner perception. Just watching her drinking water was sensual. It was indefinable, indescribable and yet it didn't need to be defined, didn't need to be described. Because in the very core that makes life, he knew things were real without question. It wasn't magic. It wasn't some psycho-mumble jumble. He knew that all things didn't need to be questioned or analyzed, for they existed always. Birds never asked why they fly—yet they did. Fish never questioned why they swam; yet they did. At six years old he never analyzed or questioned why his sister had to die, yet she did. And it was ever since then he knew you didn't have to know the reason why things and feelings existed, happened, or didn't happen, because weather you knew the answer or not they still existed. That was just the way things worked.

Heather capped her green-plastic canteen cup and placed it back on her hip. She reached down to pick up a pole just as Thomas reached for the same pole. Their hands touched, and she felt the skin on the back of his hand. She removed it—slowly. His eyes made contact with hers and she knew he wasn't looking at her--but *at her*. She smiled. Comfortably, familiarly.

"So what do you do when you're not playing army?" She questioned as they raised the pole near the tent.

He balanced the pole into position as he spoke. "I'm an artist. More to the point, I'm the art director for an advertising firm. I'm in charge of coming up with idea's, approving idea's, for various ads we run for an array of assorted clients." Once he began, he found his words kept coming and that she was genuinely listening to every one of them. "It gives me the chance to visually express myself artistically, albeit within the constraints of the product or item being advertised. On occasion, I do my own drawings and attach some poetry to it."

"Anything published that you have done on your own?"

"No. I never even thought about trying to. I've had people say I should, and that my stuff would really sell, but I was never really into that. The advertising firm pays me well enough to live the way I want to, and what I do in my personal illustrations, paintings, and writing, quells my need to express myself. To conciliate my need for acceptance, well, I live in Santa Monica right on the beach, and seeing the expanse of the ocean, the sun setting in the horizon—that's all the acceptance I think I'll ever need."

"What about you? What's the rest of your story?"

"Me!?" Heather said this as if Norby was back and he was talking to her. She hadn't thought he'd ask her, because on some level she knew he knew all about her…from before.

"Well, I told you some and I dare say the rest is nothing like yours. I graduated from the University of Southern California. I majored in mathematics. I married right after and was pregnant with a son. My husband, Bruce, had accepted a commission in the United States Army and I decided to be a stay at home mom and help Bruce in his career. At the various installations we were stationed at I taught or assisted teaching math at the school on base. When our son started school I found I had more time on my hands and Bruce convinced me to join the Army Reserve. So I guess I'm a wife, mother, and reservist all in one. And with all that, my days are filled up."

They balanced another pole under the cammo-netting.

"Yes it sounds as if your days are filled." There was pause, "but are you fulfilled?" Thomas added.

Are you fulfilled? The question reverberated in her mind. She never thought about it at least not consciously. She thought she was about to reply, *"Of course I am. Husband, kid, and a part-time career. What more do I need."* What she actually said was, "I just should be, I have a husband, kid and a part time career.

Her reply caught her by surprise, she hadn't really answered the question, and she knew Thomas knew it. But before he could reply, one of the poles came loose and began to slip. They both saw it and moved to catch it before it hit the ground. They reached it at the same time, again their hands touched, and this time his palm was on the back of her hand. He moved it away slowly. Again their eyes met and she was looking not at him but *at him*. He smiled, comfortably, familiarly. Once again the sun won the game of hide and seek with the cloud and its rays were allowed to shine. In the instant their hands touched so did the heat of the sunlight touch them-warming them.

Apologetically Heather spoke, "I know I didn't answer your question directly." As she hoisted the pole up and back into place.

He gave her a knowing smile and said, "But you did answer the question directly."

"I did?" Heather said with an eyebrow raised.

"Not in what you said, but in the way you said it."

She knew then he was listening to her. Not with his ears, but with a hearing that could detect her desires, her wishes, her dreams. She smiled at him warmly, deeply. She was comforted and scared. Her rational mind told her this wasn't happening. Could not be happening. Should not be happening. Yet this was so familiar, so right. But as we instinctively cry out the moment our lungs are filled with air at birth—thus she instinctively begged three questions of him: Who are you? Where do you come from? And why do I know you? Heather knew she asked these questions out loud, but when no reply came she realized she had given them no physical voice. She had said them, but silently, deeply, psychically. And what frightened her most was that she knew the answers – *she knew the answers*. Before another question could be asked, or another word was spoken, PFC Norby returned. "I filled up my canteen." Norby cried out as she approached. "My word. You two have been busy little bees. You're almost finished."

"Not quite," Thomas said. "We still need to anchor a few of the poles. If the wind picks up in the night I fear this won't hold."

Heather picked up a handful of rope and passed them out to Thomas and Norby. Within fifteen minutes the poles were tied securely.

Norby stepped back and took a long look at the job they had just completed. "This doesn't look very neat." What she said was true. The entire tent was covered, and none of the netting actually touched the surface of the tent. The netting dipped, curved, and bulged throughout. "I mean those other guys have there's all neat. Either squared off or lying on the tent."

"And that's exactly why they will be doing it all over again." Thomas said.

"Why?" Norby asked.

"Because it's wrong." Heather chimed in. "The reason for the netting is to make the items underneath, appear to be just another shape on the ground. The tents, vehicles, generators and the other equipment have man made shapes. The netting is put up to brake up that shape. So if we were being spied upon from the air, all our equipment would blend in and look like another terrain feature." Heather then pointed to a mountain range in the distance. "See the contours of the mountain? They dip, curve, or jut out. No real smooth or rounded off edges."

Norby's face changed as she became enlightened.

Heather noticed Thomas looking at her and smiling his approval. "Well I better go and find the First Sergeant, he's got some work to do." He tipped his hat ever so vaguely in Heather's direction as he walked away.

Norby looked at her and when she thought Thomas was out of hearing distance, she whispered, "I think the commanders hot—don't you?"

"Haven't given it much thought." Heather replied. To herself Heather smiled. She knew Norby was young and was enamored with Thomas's physical beauty. And it was that in which she replied. For as uncanny as it was, she knew this man, and what she thought about him went far beyond his corporal form.

The rest of the day passed effortlessly, as the toils of the field continued. Through digging fighting positions, setting their sector of fire, and other duties involved in organizing the base camp, Heather slyly watched Thomas. He didn't move like other men. His stride was easy, labor-less, like the walk of a jungle cat. His manner was friendly, personable, yet professional. At the border where the subconscious becomes the conscious, she dwelt in confusion. Forgetting, remembering, and forgetting, how, why, when and from where she knew this man. Just as her conscious mind would get a grip on the answer, her subconscious would snatch it back. When this happened she'd flinch—how desperately she wished she knew. She did know that this was more than happenstance, some how destiny was taking a hand.

Dusk was approaching silently and swiftly, shutting off the light of the daystar. Giving way and refocusing its illumination and casting it on earth's natural satellite. In old religions and mythology this time was special. As Heather sat eating her dinner peering at the quartz a voice across the table spoke to her. "Hey are you into crystals? Are you a crystal gazer?" Heather looked up to see the girl from the tent—the one who speculated the commander was homosexual. "No. this was given to me by someone very special to me." She said the words without thinking. After hearing them she mentally questioned herself. *"What did I say that for? What's going on? I have to get a grip."*

The girl continued, "That's too bad, I was thinking you could tell us the future." Some others at the table chuckled. Heather immediately realized she was being heckled, probably because she was new, this type of thing was so juvenile to her, but she always knew how to gain the upper hand. "Let's review that for a moment." Heather replied in a tone that a teacher would take with a student. "Can you," she looked at the girl's nametag, it read, DEVILLE. "Sergeant Deville, can you elaborate?" A wave of embarrassment bathed Deville. Her face reddened slightly. She was on the spot and felt compelled to respond. "Well, I-I was just, uhm...."

"I thought so," Heather interrupted. "It's too bad, because if you really knew what you were talking about you'd know that Crystal gazing is also called, crystallomancy or scrying. Most of you at the table may have laughed, but did you know that powerful leaders throughout history have used this medium to foretell future events and to discover knowledge?"

"That's correct." A voice interrupted from behind the soldiers. At once all seated turned in its direction and saw Major Michaels passing by. "Queen Elizabeth the first sometimes consulted the famous 17th century scryer, Doctor Dee, on matters of state. Even the legendary King Arthur sought out prophecies and advice from Merlin the Magician who was heavily involved in crystallomancy."

"Come on Sir, you don't really believe in magical and mystical happenings do you?" A husky male Sergeant questioned.

With a wicked smile, and a quick unconscious glance at Heather, then back at the sergeant, Thomas replied, "I am beginning to more and more."

Abruptly, Sergeant Deville rose from the table. Through a malevolent scowl she mockingly said, "My, aren't we the brainiac," as she looked at Heather.

Heather said nothing, just sat unsure as to why Deville was so miffed.

Leaning over close to Heather, Norby whispered, "You better watch her. I think you just made an enemy."

A few more hours passed as dusk relinquished its stay and gave way to his sibling, the darker of the two. The moon was high and shimmered white in the expanse of dusk's brother. All who were out knew for the next ten hours night would reign supreme in this part of the hemisphere. At a quarter past eight the troops were lined up and ready to begin night maneuvers.

"Sergeant Irving," First Sergeant Hillman called, "You're with the commander."

Plucking herself out of formation, she marched over to his camouflaged, cart painted Hummer.

Hillman called a few more names out and one by one the troops marched to their stations.

They all had been thoroughly briefed and conducted a reconnaissance of the area before night fully fell. Now in the darkness, save the light of the moon, they were preparing to traverse the terrain in blackout drive.

When Heather arrived at the Hummer she found Thomas looking over a map. He looked up at her seriously, timidly.

"You're my driver for this exercise?" He questioned.

"Yes, Top assigned me." She replied.

He looked at her and nodded saying, "Okay, you pilot, I'll navigate." He grinned a little.

Heather said nothing, nodded and gave him a gentle, tempered smile. She scampered into the drivers' seat. She watched Thomas walk towards the First Sergeant to confer before the start of the exercise. Heather sat back and to herself she beamed. In a few minutes she would be alone, shrouded in darkness, with an uncanny man who had stroked a cord in her that she never knew existed. She felt like she was on the edge of discovery. She was uncovering a very deep part of herself that she wasn't sure she wanted to unearth. Like raiding a mummy's tomb she was excited and afraid at the same time.

"This training will be invaluable to the troops. We constantly train in the daylight under optimum conditions. However, in time of war or conflict, things won't be ideal. I don't want anyone hurt out here but they must learn to operate their vehicles without lights, in the dark, over rough terrain." Thomas was climbing into the Hummer talking to one of his lieutenants. He closed the door. "You all set?" He said as he looked at Heather.

"Yes, sir." Heather answered but as she did she felt his blue eyes strum ever so lightly on that newly exposed string of her being.

As he looked upon Heather seated behind the steering wheel, he knew he had caressed something in her that was foreign, but yet native all the same. All morning, afternoon and now tonight he was conflicted by this women. He knew the intelligence she possessed as he pondered the intangible things he perceived about her. The acumen he sensed from her frightened him and a part of his conscious mind refused to let him believe something extraordinary was happening between them.

"The exercise will commence in the next thirty seconds." Thomas said as he checked his watch. After he spoke Heather started the engine.

"Okay, give two beeps on the horn." Thomas ordered. Heather obeyed. "You can begin driving now."

"Do I go into black out now?" Heather asked as she put the Hummer in gear.

"No, we will go out a kilometer or so, then you can turn out the lights. When the other vehicles see us go dark they'll follow."

Heather cautiously eased off the foot brake, switched to the accelerator pedal and eased the Hummer down the dirt road. She noticed how professional Thomas had sounded. How totally in charge his demeanor seemed.

"How long will we be out tonight sir?"

"I'm not sure. Top and I figured since this is our first night maybe an hour. We will do this a few more times before the two weeks are up."

"That's great. I think its good training."

"Really?" Thomas questioned not expecting a reply. "Most of the troops hate it."

"That's because they are not use to it. And you know people fear or hate what they aren't used to or understand."

Thomas smiled. "You are so right." As the irregular drone of the engine hummed and the darkness cloaked him he reflected silently on Heather. He wondered for the first time consciously, that he had real feelings connected with this women—this married women. He was feeling something, some wanting, some needing.

"So how long have you been drawing?" Heather asked as the Hummer moved ruggedly across the bumpy terrain.

"Ever since High School." Thomas replied. Then unexpectedly he laughed out loud. "The artist and the dancer."

"Excuse me?" Heather questioned.

"Oh I was just thinking about high school. My parents had died during my senior year and I guess I gravitated towards this one young lady, she was a dancer." Thomas paused and with a touch of heart-brake said, "I almost married her."

A wave of strange emotion washed over Heather as she quickly rejoiced and was saddened. She was unexplainably happy that he never had been married—still virginal in the matrimonial sense. And she was sure she felt his hurt heart and disappointment in a love lost.

She wanted to know more. Who was the young woman? Why hadn't she married him? Where was she now? Did he still communicate with her and a whole host of other questions. She suppressed her inquisitive urge and said nothing. Knowing that in part jealousy had spawned the questions. She told herself she was being ridiculous and maybe a tad selfish. She knew she should care less about the personal intricacies of Thomas's life. But she did care, and oh, how she did.

As the Hummer purred along it vibrated, and rocked, and shook to and fro from the uneven ground.

"What about you?" Thomas questioned.

"Me?"

"Yes, what was your forte in High School?"

"Math."

"Really?"

"You sound surprised."

"I guess I am a little, because most High School kids like math the least. I personally did okay. That's to say I got a B average and even then when it came to Calculus and Trigonometry I had to work at it."

"Math just came easy to me that's all." Heather replied as she glanced into the rear view mirror of the Hummer. She immediately noticed the trail vehicles disappear as she rounded a bend in the road and in that instance she thought how totally alone she was with Thomas Michaels. She noticed Thomas was looking at the foreground. The landscape was hilly and rolling, silhouetted beautifully against the night sky and a vista of mountains.

"Settling country." Thomas remarked.

Heather looked at him curiously.

"Drew up an ad for these builders a few years back, and I tell you it was as picturesque as that view ahead. The builders loved it. Said it captured the exact look and feel of everyone's dream of what the first settlers out west saw when they came to homestead, or stake their claim."

Heather looked over the landscape quickly yet meticulously taking in all the shapes and shadows. "That's real interesting. I never really gave it much thought before, but I guess if there was a little lake or water bed out there, I guess they would be right."

"Funny you should mention that, because in my painting I placed a small stream running through it." Thomas paused then said, "I love creating slices of life."

"Creating? Do you mean painting or drawing slices of life?" Heather queried.

"No. I essentially feel I create things on paper, canvass or the computer. It's a gift I have and I truly enjoy what I do. So I feel I create as opposed to imitate or reproduce something. Everything I do regardless if it's with pen, pencil, brush or whatever medium I'm working in I like to put a little of myself there, sort of embed a part of my essence, my personality, thus making my work feel alive, as though it's living and has a conscience that one will sense—on an unconscious level."

"That's a pretty tall order considering you're in advertising."

"Yes and no. Advertisement is a way to get someone to buy into what one is selling, offering or proposing. It's targeted for an average. Within those averages it is then broken down into a myriad of categories and varied demographics. I try to hit said target audience on and at their level. It's peculiar I admit but I have been successful. Then there are the works I create independently of the confines of the advertising world. Where I create images and writings that fully express my true inner self and on rare occasions some people have seen my personal creations and they have been truly amazed to the point where they urge me to publish my work."

"Why don't you." Heather asked.

"To tell you the honest truth, I feel there is something showy, and a bit narcissistic in that, because the creations were just really for me and the select few that had seen them, not so much to make a profit—whether that profit be adulation, criticism or monetary."

"That's different." Heather replied with an unconsciously raised eyebrow.

"I wouldn't really know. I get a sense that humans, not all, but the average person living in America and some places abroad want what advertisers show them; security, contentment, and what's traditional. Most of those folks are not too worried about being confronted—at least artistically or otherwise. I don't blame them really because it would start to unravel their fabric of life. They take what the advertisers impose upon them on television, movies, print ads, etc, and they shape their lives and the culture around them."

Heather reflected silently on what Thomas had said. She knew there was depth to his words. She thought about her husband and how he preached security, contentment, and tradition.

Her thoughts were interrupted as Thomas said, "Look I don't want you to get the wrong idea. I love our way of life. I wouldn't be here training to defend and preserve it if I didn't. I think this is the greatest country in the world but, on the other hand I'm a realist as well and I don't always agree to everything. I do know certain things are necessary for a society like ours to survive, prosper and continue our countries motto; life, liberty and the pursuit of happiness."

Heather smiled impressively if not surprised. She hadn't thought about life, liberty or the pursuit of happiness in a very long time, but here she was on a dark night alone with a most fascinating and strange man, for whom the things he said and thoughts were just things that went on in his mind on a daily basis. To her his words spoke volumes that were laced with truth that dare to be thought about, yet balanced with a sense that he,—the author, was not self absorbed but totally self aware of his place in the sphere of life. Bruce never talked or thought this way. Her friends didn't either. With her husband it was what was for dinner, his military investigations, Professional sport teams, or the antics of the guests of talk shows. With her friends it was the latest fashions, neighborhood and work gossip, daytime soap operas and, on occasion, something that caught their attention on the nightly news. They never talked about the fabric of life or the threads that held it together and never about artistically expressing oneself.

She drove The Hummer into what appeared to be a small valley. "Halt the vehicle here. We will give the others a second to catch up and then we will go to black out."

Heather nodded and complied.

As soon as the engine was in park Thomas exited the vehicle. She turned the engine off and departed. She immediately felt the cool, rush of night as the darkness shrouded her physical form. It was like being at home in Thousand Oaks where sometimes late into the evening after Bruce had gone to bed she would get up and go outside and experience the calm surrender of the night. She asked Bruce to join her on several occasions but he never did. The nights usually littered with illuminated constellations always made her feel alive, romantic and she had hope that Bruce would one day take her lustfully in his arms and make love to her in some cheap Harlequin novel style of romance in the darkness as the stars twinkled and watched. This never happened.

The others pulled up. Thomas began to instruct 1SG Tillman to deploy the vehicles and commence black out drive drills. He would don his night vision goggles and take notes for the next hour as each vehicle and its designated driver maneuvered the vehicles in the dark.

With the exercises under way Heather found herself next to Thomas again. This time in the night air, a gentle unpretentious casualness seemed to embrace them. They were intangibly surrounded by a hint of familiarity emitting from the nocturnal heaven itself. Driving together, sharing glimpses into each others consciousness, coupled with the strangeness of their subliminal acquaintance, intimacy was quietly starting an argument for its arrival.

He handed her his goggles. She took them and awkwardly put them on. Without saying a word Thomas reached over and fitted them perfectly around her eyes and head. To Heather the scene was odd because she usually could out soldier any guy, but around Major Thomas Michaels she fell to pieces. With the goggles on, they immediately took in and refracted every bit of light found in the sky. She took several steps forward. Everything she viewed was radiant, and majestically clear but in greenish hue. She saw the vehicles silhouetted against the horizon lumbering across the terrain. Even a few fireflies flickering in and around their position. The moon had changed into an emerald orb. Heather looked across the entire scenery and back at Thomas, a man who seemed to belong and blend into the scenery of her being.

"Kind of gives you a different perspective looking at things through jade color goggles." He said walking towards her. "You actually hear things differently when you see them differently." He said this last line as he effortlessly removed the goggles and wiped at her eyes.

"Hear things differently?" She pondered his last sentence. Within seconds she silently agreed with him. She looked over the landscape once more. Now free of the goggles everything look different, all the colors of the rainbow were back and shaded in varying degrees of black as opposed to green, but things sounded different as well. Just like when you listen to a foreigner. At first you hear the accent and not so much what they say, but as you hang round them and become more familiar,

Memories, Light, & Promise

you see them from another perspective. Thus not noticing the accent, Thus hearing them differently.

Not bothering to put on the goggles or look at the vehicles Thomas strode towards the Hummer with Heather at his side. "Okay, if I'm not being too intrusive, and do tell me if I am, can you tell me more about yourself." They had just reached the Hummer. He placed the goggles on the hood, leaned his elbow on it and stared at her.

"Intrusive! How could you ever think such a thing?" This thought ran through her mind, as she said, "I like talking to you."

He smiled. Even in the moonlight sky she knew the smile said, "Ditto."

She began by telling him about her years as an only child. Her Christian upbringing, and her parents, both of whom were retired and living in Kansas. She told him about life on the farm with them, her excelling in math and a dream to leave the small town and go to college. She chronicled her time at USC, some of the guys and about meeting and eventually marrying Bruce and becoming a part of the Army Reserve.

Thomas listened. She could tell just by his body language, nod of the head, a smile or frown, even the shift in his stance that he understood and wasn't passing judgment on anything she talked about. She did hesitate a moment when it came to the part about Bruce and their son.

The hesitation came in response to her innocence. An innocence impregnated and birthed in the subconscious recesses of her own romanticism about her connection to Thomas—what was—what is—what will be. Yet before the proverbial slap on the posterior, the hesitation was over and she spoke confidently about Bruce and her son—at least consciously she did. He already knew Bruce was in the military, it was their son Toby, ten, in the fifth grade and the spitting image of his father that he learned about.

"While I'm here for two weeks, Bruce's parents will shuttle him back and forth to school and Bruce will pick him up in the evening." She knew the exercise was nearing its end and so would their conversation. Maybe Thomas would continue when they got back, maybe he would thank her for her time then dismiss himself. He was noble; she sensed he was a dreamer but, kind, gentle and even a tad reserved.

33

Five minutes after these thoughts washed over her she saw the lights of the vehicles flash to life. The horizon was now bathed in white light and visible dust clouds as the vehicles now headed toward their position. Heather took this as her signal to wrap things up. Their casualness dissipated and the silent embrace was no more. She took one affectionate betraying look at Major Thomas Michaels, artist, writer, dreamer, realist, half of a twin. Noticing his look was just as affectionate as hers.

1SG Tillman had returned. The two men professionally discussed a closing formation and the procedures for bedding down. Heather now sat in the Hummer. Looking towards the expanse of the blackened atmosphere, she felt awake, fully awake as though she had been Rip-Van Wrinkle and her twenty year sleep was on the brink of being over. Heather Irving was Thirty-four year's old coming out of a dream and couldn't wait for her passenger to enter her vehicle and drive with her.

3
Memories - Part 1

They had driven back to the campsite mostly in silence. As they approached the area Heather thought, *"I don't want this to end."*

"It won't. Not yet." Thomas replied.

"Excuse me?" Heather said in complete surprise.

"I was responding to your comment."

Heather knew she hadn't said a word, not out loud. Was Thomas able to read her thoughts? Who was this man? As she replied the crystal quartz in her pocket warmed. "But I didn't say anything."

Thomas smiled warmly, and looked deeply in her hazel green eyes. "I know."

Heather abruptly and instinctively slammed on the breaks. The Hummer stopped, they were at the site, and without another word between them Thomas exited. Heather sat back in her seat in a cold sweat and she quivered. It was eerie and exciting at the same time. In the moment Thomas looked at her and spoke, something happened. It was quick, paroxysmal in nature and unmistakable—she experienced an orgasm.

Within ten minutes Heather found herself in formation standing with Norby and a grimacing Deville. "I see you getting all cozy with the commander." Deville whispered to her.

Heather looked the twenty-two year old up and down and dismissed her with out saying a word.

The formation broke and she and Norby walked towards the tent.

"What is Deville's problem?" Heather questioned, more than a little agitated.

"Don't really know, during the exercise I heard some of the guys talking. They said her father is the IG at the headquarters."

"Inspector General?"

"Yeah, so Deville thinks she's hot shit."

"You must be joking? Who cares who her father is?"

"I'm just telling you."

"I'll meet you at the tent later. I'm going to get some juice from the mess tent."

"Okay."

Heather stood for a moment and watched Norby head for the tent. She thought about Thomas. Looking in the direction of his tent, she rejected the thought of seeking him out.

Thomas was frightened. He sat in the mess tent sipping some tea. He was alone and trying to calm himself. Thomas was wondering about Heather and how in the hell did he have the ability to read her thoughts, finish her sentences—a women he had never met until today, yet he felt as though he had known her all his life. He prided himself on being a realist but this was unreal. It was as if this was another time, another place. As he reminisced about her and how she had spoken to him at the hood of the Hummer in the benevolence of the night fall—he had watched her, and tried hard to remember something that never happened—or did it. Then a thought came to him in a whisper, *Today will be Yesterday.* Thomas looked up quickly just as Heather entered the tent.

"Sir?" Heather questioned in consternation. "Is that you?" The question was rhetorical, she knew the answer even though Thomas was seated and shaded by the shadows.

Thomas didn't answer; he knew she knew it was him. Sounding professional, yet personal he said, "Sergeant Irving lets go walk-about." He rose and walked towards her. She was ten paces away and with each step he fought himself. Step 1—Just ask her who she is; 2—You know who she is; 3—Ask her why she's here; 4—You know why she's here;

5—Just kiss her; 6—she's married; 7—she's married to you; 8—Is she my past?; 9—She's your future; 10—This can't be happening; As he reached her he held the flap of the tent back for her then followed her outside.

They headed towards the ravine where he had found the crystal. They crossed the matted grass, over the dirt path and onto the uneven ground. He took her hand as they descended "Is this a gully?" She asked.

Thomas paused, "Yeah, I think it is. This trench is here because running water carved the earth up like this, and I think when it rains water still flows through here. *Why would she want to know that? He questioned himself.*" But he did know why, *she was always inquisitive, that's why math was so easy for her. She liked to figure things out and have the exact meaning.* As his mind seized upon this information he was bewildered. And then it came again in yet another whisper carried by his memories, *Today will be Yesterday.*

"I beg your pardon?" Thomas stated.

"I didn't say anything." Heather replied.

Thomas looked up as if to ask the heavens and God for strength. He saw the moon, lit up for all in this hemisphere to see, along with its cousins, and its other stellar relatives twinkling around it.

He had much on his mind, and much more in his heart. Often he would walk on the beach at night but never could he see the stars—for the lights of the city. It was here, now, with this women as if a veil had been lifted and revealed something they both had known and knew, that he/she was educated, intelligent, and well versed in the ways of learned social decency, behavior and morality. How many times had he/she mentally sneered, or condemned, cultural deviancy, adulterated acts, indecent innuendos and the likes? But here he was struggling against something primal, hormonal, psychological, and unexplainable and found themselves at the precipice of each. For them the battle was not to fall over. And for that sake alone he fought his nature, as she fought hers.

"Must keep this civil," he told himself. "Moons' Full tonight." He remarked.

She smiled, "Moons' been full for several nights. You know what they say."

And simultaneously they said, "Strange things happen when the moon is full." Immediately they both began to laugh. It was a good laugh, a comforting laugh, a laugh that broke dimensions, shattered time and in that moment, *today became yesterday*

* * *

They were no longer in a gully at Camp Pendleton, CA on a Reserve Annual Training Exercise. They were back in time—their past, their memories—together laughing, in love and sharing life. He chased her and she chased him in a time when they had each other. They were alike yet different. In the laughter they both realized it, for a fraction of a mille-second it had reach their conscious mind and poof, like a forgotten dream it was gone.

"You know if I were at home I would probably be outside reading right about now."

"It's pretty late for a read is it not?" Thomas questioned.

"No, not for me. After preparing, eating, then cleaning up after dinner, to say nothing of listening to one of Bruce's cases, and helping Toby with his homework, I find I can really enjoy myself reading on a starry night."

"If I've had a hectic week at work, sometimes on the weekends I leave the city and paint the stars." He moved close to her, placed his hand on her shoulder as though this move was common for them and pointed upward.

"You see that?" Thomas asked.

"The cluster of stars? The little dipper?" Heather questioned.

"Yes and no." Thomas replied, "The pole star, at the tip of the handle of Ursa Minor."

Heather looked, remembering that Ursa Major–the Big Dipper was the easiest way to find the pole star because two of its stars were directly in line with the North Star. "I got it." Heather replied.

"Well the pole star is a directing principle."

"As well as a center of attraction." She replied.

Time stood still once more and again *today became yesterday.*

The tug, the pull of knowledge, an awaking, a discovery—each moment, each thought was bringing them closer—alike, yet different. They both stood motionless and in that instant there was excitement, wonderment and recognition. They both were excited at the prospect of being together mentally, emotionally, physically. They wondered how evenly matched they were mentally from Astronomy to Crystallomancy. They both recognized the sameness, the familiarity between them, though they were perfect strangers.

To Heather, Thomas seemed to come from some far off constellation, talked like it, thought like it, acted and moved like it.

To Thomas, Heather was his pole star, his center of attraction. There was another term for it a mathematical term from calculus. It escaped him for the moment—he would remember later.

The instant was fleeting and like water on cotton candy it was gone.

They walked in the ravine for a few kilometers, and circled around the campsite. They were alone. All the troops were in their tents. No one seemed to be stirring not even the field rodents. "This is a dancing night." Heather said unexpectedly. This took her totally by surprise.

"*What?*" She questioned silently as her face reddened.

Thomas smiled, his warm smile, the one that said I understand. It eased her embarrassment.

In her moment of lost composure he felt her, the essence of her and that triggered something sexual within him. He wanted her. For the first time since he looked upon her, spoke to her, became imperceptibly in tuned with her, he consciously wanted to touch her beautiful red hair, trace his fingers across the curves and slopes of her shoulders, back and waist. He wanted to feel his mouth on her mouth, lips, tongue. He reflected on how he would feel inside her—how they would dance.

He fought these thoughts. He was the commander of this unit, she was married, and they had responsibilities. He had to change perspectives quick. Look at it another way so he could *hear* something else.

"Well I haven't danced in a long time myself. I've been asked to go to several clubs in Los Angeles, but I always pass." Heather responded.

This worked. His hormonal urges subsided—momentarily.

Heather smiled, her warm smile. The smile that said, "You know what I mean but, I thank you for being a gentleman."

And that's when it came back. It was in the pout of her lips, the softness of her eyes, the loose locks of hair under her cap—the way she looked. He wanted to feel her fingers across his chest, down his stomach, between his legs, her naked body pressed softly, tenderly, lovingly against his.

The urge was strong he wanted to act, needed to act, felt he was compelled to act. But he was stronger than that. This after all was something born of himself, he would control it. He would fight it; he would not let it come to disclosure. There were rules and he knew them well. There was a long pause as he stretched his body hard in an attempt to physically pummel and repel the urges and thoughts out of his mind.

Heather knew Thomas was in a fight with himself. She felt his pain, his denial and his longing. It was in his eyes where she was incessantly caught in his vision. He tried not to be apparent—and he wasn't. He tried not to be invasive—he succeeded. She knew this because they were kindred spirits connected a long time ago, wrapped in anonymity. And she wanted him too.

She knew, he knew, she hadn't danced in a long time even though she was married. She also knew that he hadn't danced in a long time even though he was single. For both it was unfortunate, borderline tragic, and full of emptiness. She knew he was strong. His strength radiated even more as he fought against the pangs that now battled his principles.

"You know what? I could use a stiff drink right about now." Thomas said.

With a demure manner and a tone, Heather questioned him with one word. "Really?"

"Really!" Thomas replied as he slipped in to congeniality. "Yes every now and then I have a small drink, vodka, cognac, even rum."

"Bruce, like most men drank Jack Daniels and beer, but I sip on cognac myself on occasion." Heather replied.

A cool ocean breeze blew in and seemed to coddle them for a moment as if the forces of nature really liked these two and stopped to say hello and in that moment Thomas raised an invisible glass and beckoned Heather to do the same. She did and proposed a toast, "Today will be yesterday." She didn't know why she said it but it seemed appropriate. Their invisible glasses touched and they swallowed their imaginary drinks.

Heather was in an emotional rapture she had only fantasized about. She was with a handsome stranger, on a starry night, telling stories and feeling feelings she long since forgot. Here she was Heather Irving, wife of Bruce and mother to Toby, actually enjoying herself with another man. A mystery of a man, a man she knew as well as herself, and yet not at all. *"How is this even possible?"* She questioned silently.

She took a short quick breath looked into Thomas' eyes and said, "There's a two drink minimum soldier."

Once again they raised their invisible glasses, this time the toast was silent and they drank once more. Anyone who saw them may have gotten the wrong idea. She knew it was about time to turn in.

As a product of the supernatural bond they shared right from the start he said, "As much as I enjoy your company, it's late and high time I head to my tent and you to yours."

She was satisfied and thankful. She was also disenchanted. It was as though she was Cinderella, and she had been given time to spend with the handsome prince, now the clock was striking twelve. "Please stay just a little longer?" She pleaded inside herself.

If Thomas had been able to read her thoughts she heard no evidence of it in his reply. "We have a big day tomorrow; have to prepare for weapons qualification."

"You must be kidding? How can you think of weapons qualifications now?" Heather begged silently. Out loud she said, *"Yes that's a big task, safety and all that, have to be well rested."*

Again silently she said, "What are you doing, I know you feel this connection between us. Major Thomas Michaels don't go not yet, at least tell me what you're really thinking." This time she clutched the crystal it was not warm but hot in her hands.

Thomas walked towards her and placed his two hands on her shoulders. "There's something about you that I just don't understand, and to tell you the truth I don't want to. Thank you for being you. Thank you for joining this unit, being my driver this night and sharing your time with me. It has been unexpectedly pleasurable and quite grand."

He was blushing in the moonlight. She couldn't see that his face had become beet red but she knew it all the same. She could also tell he was genuinely sincere—it was in his voice.

He continued, "You're a very good person, Heather. You ought to have that husband of yours take you out dancing and often, if I was him I would."

She smiled, it was her knowing smile. The crystal was burning and her clairvoyance, mystical insight, whatever it was she was positive he knew all about her. She welcomed his words knowing he had the best intentions for her. He knew physical romance had some how became foreign to her, along with a host of other intimate things. He meant for her to have it, it was in his tone—soft, it was in his touch on her shoulders—gentle. It was in what he didn't say, "You should go home, beat your husband, or leave him. He has to be an idiot not to see all your beauty—your total qualities."

"You'll make it to your tent okay?" He asked.

"Yes."

"I could walk you."

She smiled the thank you smile. "That won't be necessary sir."

"Well, good night." He said this as he slowly walked to his tent.

Heather stood there locked in shadow and light, watching as he walked away in the darkness, he didn't disappear all at once, he just seemed to become dim, dimmer, and then dimmest until he was no longer physically visible. When he was gone the moon itself seemed to fade and everything didn't seem as radiant as it just was.

Heather made her way back to her tent; she wasn't aware of the time and didn't care. She moved quietly among the rows of cots and carefully reached hers without disturbing the sleeping women. She removed her boots, and uniform. Covered by the darkness deep within the shadows of the female filled tent she stood in her bra and panties. She smoothed her hands over her breasts, they were full, firm and just the right size for her build. She traced her hands in the darkness over her stomach and hips. Her stomach was flat from her daily sit-up routine and there was firmness and tone around her waist. She sat and rubbed her legs, which were hairless, thanks to genetics, and tight and femininely muscular, thanks to forty-five minutes a day on a treadmill in her home. She never consciously worked on her body to keep toned and nice, it was just part of her job in the Reserve to pass a Bi-annual Physical Training test, and she had always ate a modest diet. Nonetheless for some reason in the past few years Bruce didn't seem interested in touching her. Sex was seldom, maybe twice a quarter and even then it was uneventful, short, and sometimes not worth the effort.

But Bruce was a good provider, a great father, never boozed it up, womanized, or hit her, and he had the best intentions for her. She respected and appreciated that. Until this morning, this day, and this night, that had always seemed to be enough for her. The slice of herself that dreamt of pleasurable sex, the wanting to be pampered and fussed over, stimulated and challenged, caressed and stroked, fed and communed with physically was suppressed. Bruce could never give her these things. He loved her, but he wasn't her *true love,* and she wasn't his.

Heather eased herself into her Army green goose-down feathered stuffed sleeping bag and said her prayers. And as she drifted off to sleep she couldn't escape the thought of Major Thomas. For some unexplainable, indefinable, and mixed up reason she knew he loved her, and knew how to please all the slices of her, he always did.

It was then Heather sat up unzipping her sleeping bag. She peeled her self out of it and reached inside her pant pocket. She retrieved the crystal; it was cool, no where near as hot or warm as it once was. She clutched it tight as she enveloped herself back into her olive drab cocoon. Holding the crystal fist tight on her chest and feeling the piece of quartz heat up she calmly closed her eyes and whispered softly to Thomas. It was a few seconds later when she mentally received his reply.

4
Memories - Part 2

The daystar had yet to illuminate the Southern California coast as Major Thomas Michaels strode past the female tent. He was in search of the First Sergeant and a cup of java. His mind was on a Starbucks Café Americano but knew the mess boys served instant coffee. He slowed his stride as he looked in the direction of the mass of green canvass, and silently cursed himself. He was irritated with himself, Heather, her husband—especially with her husband. "If you have a dancing partner that lovely, you dance."

Heather shifted in her sleeping bag at the very moment Thomas passed. Still asleep with her fist clutching the crystal she could see Thomas walking and slowing. She listened to his thoughts and whispered in response, "It's not your fault." Her retort was never voiced out loud but she knew he heard her. They were linked subconsciously and that's where she spoke to him.

He entered the mess tent knowing the mess sergeant was already adding hot water to the dehydrated product made from brewed coffee.

"Looks like you need this more than I do." First Sergeant Hillman said as he handed him a cup.

"Thanks," Thomas said as he took it. "You about ready?"

"That's an affirmative." He picked up a silver thermos, patted it. "I have more and the Hummer is ready, Sir."

After a long sip he said, "Then let's hit it." Thomas gave a little greeting nod in the direction of the mess sergeant and his help then exited. He shifted his cup and zipped up his GORTEX camouflaged field jacket. He walked quietly behind Hillman and entered the Hummer.

On the drive out to the range he wished he was being driven by Heather.

"It's going to be a long day today sir."

"Everyday seems long these days."

"Amen to that. The detail I put together won't be out for another hour or so."

"Good. That will give me time to ensure everything is all set up."

Range Fire was an exercise he took very seriously. He didn't want to have an accidental death on his hands. He was aware that reservist rarely handled live ammunition and he hadn't been able to do the walk through with range control due to some work obligations. Though the fulltime staff, Hillman and his platoon leaders had briefed him and prepared an operations order, he wanted to physically visit the site ahead of the troops. This was just to make sure every thing was in order because, as the commander of the unit, ultimately he was responsible if anything went wrong.

The range was dusty and barren, yet off in the hills surrounding it vegetation and wildlife was abundant. Deer, Bison and even wild boar roamed freely through the hills and the foliage of Camp Pendleton. Thomas thought about this and hoped none of them wandered over here today. If any soldier so much as killed a field mouse the Environmental Protection Agency would swear they started World War III. He chuckled to himself about the strict sanctions the EPA had on this land, and the dichotomy of having to train soldiers on it as well.

Once out at the range he and Tillman walked the grounds going over everything and how it would be laid out. His intent was to qualify his troops on the M16A-2 Rifle and the Crew Served Weapon, the M60 machine gun. This was a little more intense than just bringing the soldiers out for weapons familiarization. He had already decided Nuclear, Biological, and Chemical (NBC) training would be part of the exercise. His troops would fire and qualify in full MOPP gear; Mask, suit, and boots the whole works. Single Channel Ground Air Radio System would also be trained with as they used mounted radios as a means of communication on the ranges.

Two different ranges were going to be occupied. The first range was for the M16 Assault Rifle's and the other for the M60 Machine Gun's.

He knew to get a quality firing; things would run into the next day, Sunday. He checked his watch, the detail had another thirty minutes to show up and actually establish the range. LT Schafer was his range Officer In Charge (OIC). He had no intention of micro managing Schafer. Once he arrived he would go over a few details and then step aside.

"Top, the MRE's?"

"The Meals Ready to Eat will be issued during the breakfast meal."

"Check. Make sure there's a hot meal waiting at the end of the day."

"Roger that, Sir."

Thomas looked at his clip board and the names and number of soldiers that needed to qualify.

As he looked over the roster he came across Heather's and paused. It was a new day and this woman still haunted his thoughts. Suddenly he remembered something, something in his subconscious that briefly broke free to his conscious mind. It was a request that came to him late last night after he had retired to his tent. It was all hazy to him but he knew he promised to do what she had asked. Thomas quickly put it out of his mind for now and continued checking the names.

A few minutes later he called for Hillman, "Top I need you to walk to the base of the tower with me and the firing line."

"Gonna check the firing points?" Hillman questioned.

"Roger that."

Still looking at the list they checked how many number of soldiers would be at each site, by firers, assistant firers, and support personnel. Next stop was the ammunition point. He went over the list of the qualified ammo handlers and the spec's for the vehicle designated for transporting the ammo. Soon the detail showed up, LT Schafer his

Non-commissioned Officer In Charge (NCOIC) and seven soldiers. They brought two water buffalo's with them.

The first thing Thomas checked was to see if Schafer had brought all his training documentation.

"Sir I have the following; Map Series V8995 (Camp Pendleton MIM South) edition 2/DM

1980 Scale 1:31,500; Operation Plan, AR 385 63, DA PAM 350-38, Standards in Weapons Training, and our Risk Assessment for this exercise."

He nodded approvingly, "Remember Bradley, Marksmanship is about precision and confidence."

Thomas reminded the Lieutenant.

"Sir, each range will have an Armorer who comes equipped with a weapons maintenance kit. I and my team will ensure that each soldier's weapon is zeroed, before they qualify."

Thomas already knew this and just nodded his approval. "Hip pocket training?" He questioned

"As briefed during our last admin, it has been planned out. There are more than enough tasks to fill in the gaps of any down-time on the ranges."

He knew Schafer had covered all of this and more in their last administrative meeting but he just wanted to double check. This went on for another thirty minutes as every detail was discussed from all ten classes of supply to every service and support item. Then Thomas and Hillman boarded the Hummer and headed back to the campsite where they would address the morning formation. On the way back Thomas noticed there were no cumulus vapors about, and knew the game of hide and seek between the sun and the clouds would not take place today. As he neared the campsite he also noticed how anxious he had become—it was Heather. He wanted to see her—didn't want to see her. *"Come on, Thomas old boy,"* He told himself, *"You have to shake this women. She's married, for goodness sake and not really unhappily married, with a kid to boot. I don't care what you feel, or what you think you know, leave this alone. You're intelligent enough to know, no one needs the risks and complications involved. Ignore the mystical implications; forget about yesterday and yester night."* Try as he might his angst grew and he was losing to his subconscious mind. *"There is something so dammed familiar, so unbelievably comfortable about her. She's more than lovely, more than special, we are connected. I can read her thoughts, she mine—but how, why?"*

Heather had washed, dressed and eaten. She now stood in formation listening to Hillman call out the firing order and to her surprise and delight she was in the first group. She knew there was nothing worse than going out all day and having to fire last. She thought she would get a chance to see Thomas, but she did not. Heather assumed he was off exerting his quiet power, on the behalf of the unit.

Heather couldn't have been more correct. One of the reasons he was a good commander was because he was a good leader. He knew how to step aside and trust his people. He let Hillman take the formation while he collected and sent the morning personnel and equipment status reports back to Headquarters.

Forty-five minutes later Thomas found himself in front of the formation and back at the range. It was his responsibility to conduct the safety brief before the start of the range fire. What he told them was short, simple and to the point and said with deadly seriousness. "Safety is paramount to everything we do. Nothing we do in peace is worth the life of a soldier. Do I make myself clear."

All one hundred and twenty seven soldiers responded with a hearty, and loud, "Yes, Sir."

Thomas paused, then smiled and softened his tone, "Oh and by they way when dealing with indigenous species e.g. snakes, insects, etc. don't or you won't be safe from me."

Everyone laughed.

Thomas turned the formation over to Hillman who immediately began calling out the serial order of fire. As he saw Heather file out and form the first order he remembered her late night mental request. *"Would you write me a poem?"* He remembered his reply, *"Yes."* He began to smile to himself a little as he imagined the bond they shared, where she could send him mental messages and he would actually, could actually receive them. Twenty minutes after the first rounds were fired down range, Thomas found himself back at the campsite and in his tent. He was rambling through his foot locker looking for his artists pens and paper. As he did he couldn't help but wonder about this mysterious woman. He was slowly losing a battle he had been purposely and consciously fighting all morning. He knew as the commander, all eyes were on him. Each troop, young, or old, new or seasoned took their cue from him. If he did anything unethical, illegal or immoral the act would spread through the unit like wild fire. He knew if he did anything with Heather it would be a mistake. A mistake in the back of his mind he was willing to make, but he knew it wasn't right or fair to Heather. Although this was something extraordinary, unfathomable and totally cosmic between them, there would be no way to explain that to anyone that hadn't experienced this kind of affinity for and with another. They'd throw the bible and morality up as their first and last line of defense. Thomas knew he himself wouldn't have understood it—if it wasn't happening to him. Due to the nature of his job and his life experiences, he never underestimated the excitement and enjoyment people received from hearing idle gossip, and trivial personal information about other people, especially if the person being chit-chatted about were in a role of responsibility. This was reinforced every time television ratings or magazine sales soared after a political scandal was exposed; a football celebrity killed his wife or a hundred other non consequential escapades that took place involving public figures. However, talk about warring tribes in the Middle East, hungry people in third world nations, or the aids epidemic, and most people wouldn't tune in or let it touch their consciousness. Thomas knew the troops of his unit were a slice, a cross section of the populace at large and it would be news indeed if Major Thomas Michaels, military officer was interacting in a personal manner with Sergeant First Class Heather Irving, a noncommissioned officer and married woman. After all there were laws against that. The rumors would commence as a trickle: something to be wondered about; then becoming a stream: something to be talked about; then grow to be a flood: something to be investigated; then developing into an ocean: something huge to be exposed for all to see and comment on. Thomas knew this is how it was, from the beginning of time, born deep in the recesses of the cerebral cortex, for reasons known and unknown, translucent and opaque. For these reasons and for Heathers' sake he needed to leave this alone. *"Like eve should have done with the apple."* he thought. It was this last thought that stirred something deep with in him, and as if inspired in some bewitching way he began to feverishly compose a poem—one that would change everything.

It was midday before Thomas had returned to the firing range. Once there he was briefed by LT Schafer that two firing orders were complete and three orders remained. He was given the score sheets of the soldiers that had qualified. "The scores aren't bad." He thought as he counted the number of Marksman, Sharpshooters and Experts. After he finished with Schafer he went out and talked to the soldiers and ensured they were drinking enough water. It wasn't long before he spied Heather. She was alone as she filled up her canteen at the water point. Thomas decided to walk over.

"Well, I see someone's making sure they stay hydrated." He kindly remarked, as he neared the water point.

Heather almost dropped the canteen in surprise. A welcomed spark was set off that ignited something all through her. It was something warm and wonderful, something in her past, something in her memories long forgotten.

"I wrote you a poem, as you requested. I don't have it with me, so I'll have to give it to you later. "That's if it's still okay?"

"Of course it wasn't okay," Heather thought, she wanted the poem now. She was dying to know what he wrote. "It's okay." She replied against her will. "I didn't think you'd get around to it so soon. Besides, I wouldn't want to read out here. I'd wait until I was off the range and in a comfortable place."

Then he added, "I can arrange for you to go back to the campsite."

Heather's eyes brightened then dimmed, as she turned this over in her head. She wanted to leave. She wanted to leave with him. *"But what if people started speculating? Already Deville seemed to be harboring some animosity towards her. It was impossible but what if the mere hint of impropriety got back to Bruce?"* To her she seemed to take along time to respond when in reality it wasn't even two seconds. "I'd love to go back to the campsite."

Thomas smiled, "Good I'll talk with the First Sergeant and you and a few others will." Heather smiled, "Then later it is."

Heather watched as Thomas talked to Hillman. She imagined he asked for a detail of people comprised of the first firing order, or something. It wasn't more than twenty minutes later she heard her name called with others to load the truck to return to the campsite.

Upon her return Heather and the others were instructed to clean up, change uniforms and be prepared to help with the evening meal. They were given two hours to take showers and get the dirt from the range off of them and then report to the mess tent.

It was hot—late fall hot and the cool water spraying from the showerhead felt great across her skin. As Heather soaped and washed herself she had a strong sense of Thomas, as though he was near, watching her, drawing her, she subconsciously invited him to join her—to become the water and cascade across her breasts, abdomen, buttocks, down and through her legs.

She had showered, dried and re-clothed and was now heading towards the mess tent, when she was approached by a somewhat sullen Major Thomas. *"What's wrong?"* She thought. *"He's coming to tell me he didn't write the poem."* Then as he reached her she asked, "Are you okay?"

"I'm fine, it's just that I have something to say to you." He made a pregnant pause, then continued, "I don't want you to get the wrong idea."

Heather looked questioningly at him, trying to search his mind telepathically—nothing.

"It's just that, me writing the poem, getting you off the range and all, well considering our ranks, my position, your marital status, coupled with the fact that we are not alone here in the unit troops might talk and ..." He trailed off, paused then said, "I don't want you to feel pressured, like I'm coming on to you or anything."

Heather knew what he was trying to say, yet she stood silently, eyes wide as he finished.

"What I'm saying is that I may have made an oversight with my actions and if you don't want me to do any of this don't be afraid to tell me."

She knew he was just being sensitive to her; this was just a part of who he was, and how he was. She wanted to hug him right there, but she just smiled, it was her don't be ridiculous smile. Then she said, "I think you know me better than that, but thank you just the same."

Her smile became bigger as she tenderly and confidently said, "I want my poem."

"Soon as you're through with your detail, and I have something else I'm working on."

"Great." She responded as she headed off in the direction of the mess tent.

"Okay, you are putting yourselves out there I hope you two can handle the risk?" Thomas questioned himself silently. Intimacies argument became more profound, and though dangers were involved, as well as, moral turpitude, Heather and Thomas consciously knew possibility was making its way into the fray.

Heather was now convinced, Thomas's sincerity and chivalry was undeniable. Almost immediately she found the being of the man, the inner part of his soul, the struggling of his spirit and the effort to do the right thing, she found it all intensely erotic. Something as casual as their conversation and the way they communicated felt so pleasing, so right. Why didn't she and Bruce interact this way? Her literal mind knew the answer; most men in this society were raised, and influenced by a culture that told them how to act and how to behave as a quote unquote MAN. From the magazines, to the television shows, to misinterpretations in the bible, men of many societies were trained to be tough, to be strong. They were taught to show no emotions, no weakness, to have all the answers. If they violated these edicts then they are labeled weak, soft, unmanly. And in relationships, if you look hard enough, you would find they have roles, predictable roles, i.e., it's a mans job to take out he trash, a man's job to wash the car, etc, etc, and thus the dichotomy; Men become banal, in a way that is both comforting, and yet restraining. She knew this wasn't true of all men, but Bruce was doing all he could, working eight hours a day, clothing, and feeding her and Toby, doing his best to take care of all of their needs the best he knew how. And dealing with life, a wife, children, and ones own personal and professional demands, made a man spread himself thin, as he tired to juggle so many things, to make every one happy and keep them entertained, but sooner or later the audience would tire of the juggling act and want something else, and at the same time ridicule the man if he drops any of the balls he is currently keeping afloat.

But with Bruce it was deeper than that, she had spoken to him often about her feelings and her thoughts, but he was afraid, afraid, that he wouldn't or couldn't fulfill her inner desires. So change never came, and change wouldn't come. Not with sex, not with his touch, and not with the inner erection, that would break barriers in his mind that would unleash his true passion. Thus the true fulfillment and the potential of their marriage would never be reached, and intimacy would always be longing. Why couldn't men be like Thomas, sensitive, strong, artistic, and yet pleasing and gentle in bed. Heather hadn't been to bed with Thomas, not physically, but mentally, emotionally, she experienced things with this man that told of a union of their flesh that would rival anything suggested at in any women's magazine. She was tired of going through the ritual of Bruce's desires, as her face was on the pillow, and he doing his best to please, she endured, knowing soon it would be over and then sleep would rescue her from the weight and discomfort of his body. She didn't know how she knew, but she knew that Thomas Michaels understood her, all of her, and his weight would be worth the wait.

The day had been engulfed by her eager counter part, and now unbound, like a raging hormone it let its dark nature loose on the world. It was 9 PM. when Heather with a lax mane entered Thomas's tent. Due to the humidity in the night sky she had a budding sheen of perspiration upon her. Add in the mysteries of the shadows and Heather looked sultry—Latin sultry. She was wearing her PT uniform, the gray shirt looked black in the light of the tent, and the same light picked up every subtle muscularity of her tread-milled legs, as they were exposed from the border of her shorts.

Thomas was seated and stood instinctively as she entered. He moved toward her smoothly like a jungle cat, not as though he was stalking prey, but as he was moving toward a fellow huntress. As he caught the silhouetted interspersed outline of her face, arms and legs he let out a soft, mental jungle cry—she smiled in the darkness, it was her I'm glad you like what you see smile. Thomas stretched out his firm muscular arm and handed her a sheet of parchment that had calligraphy scrawling all over it. With emotions as electric as Aladdin rubbing the lamp for the first time their feelings soared. The minute her fingers touched the paper, all the emotion, all of the cogitating, all of the seeking, seemed to let the genie out. Everything now came to the fore—their past was their memories. Unspoken, yet now known was the truth. In their conscious mind they accepted the reality—as impossible and improbable as it may have come about—they were in love. Army Reserve Major Thomas Michaels, Commander of the 69th Quartermaster Company, half of a twin, professional artist and self-styled poet was in love with Heather Irving. With admiration that Narcissus had for himself, and/or that the peasants had for Athena, Thomas, in a voice that echoed true reverence everything he felt came through as he said, "This is for you."

Every molecule in Heathers body, every nerve running up and down her spinal cord and every hair on the nape of her neck was on edge. Before he could lead her to the dim light to read the poem, she was swirling a cosmic, self defining internal spin. In her hands the poem seemed to glow white hot, but she couldn't let go. Hidden deep in her foot locker the quartz crystal was burning mystically, and melting.

The poem was twenty lines, five stanzas of four and she read it, without reading it. The words were written with exacting skill and a knowledge that stifled all reason. The poem made no sense, and yet it made perfect sense. She immersed herself in the feeling of it, the explanation of it, and the tale of it. She let the totality of it, the awfulness of it, the redemption of it take her, each line was absorbed in all her apertures, the ones real and imagined, the ones opened in her past—the memories, the ones opened now in her present—the light, and the ones that would be opened in her future—the promises yet to be fulfilled. It was as though she was dead, and now like Lazarus, being raised from the eternal slumber. She was alive again and in her hand was the permission slip, the catalyst that made her resurrection permissible, possible and acceptable. It was the realization of love—true love that was preparing Sergeant Heather Irving, Army Reserve non-commissioned officer, Mother of Toby, and wife of Bruce, ready to *Bite into the apple.*

5
Light – Part 1

Bite Into the Apple

Though promised to another, it is we that are kindred.
A relationship that's known in our
hearts again and again.
Unlike Adam and Eve in that garden called Eden,
Indulging in the apple that is our love will not be a sin.

From my rib you did not manifest, but we are
Connected in a way that's very uncanny, yet real.
To hear tell of our affinity would seem forbidden,
But, no serpents tongue will change the way we feel.

The way for us seems to be blocked by religion and man,
Frightened of the consequences of our feelings and fate
Thus an exodus, from the haven of
things that keep us safe.

> **3**
> **Sacrificing the experience to taste the love of a soul-mate.**
>
> **Like in genesis we are balanced, only**
> **but watching the apple.**
> **A bite will upset this revealing our**
> **nakedness—it's shame or glory.**
> **It will not be easy, we will be judged,**
> **but together we'll be**
> **filled with knowledge, taking on all**
> **and making our own history.**
>
> **Though promised to another, it is we that are kindred.**
> **A relationship that's known in our**
> **hearts again and again,**
> **Now similar to Adam and Eve in the garden called Eden,**
> **Bite into the apple, because we too shall be forgiven.**

As Heather's eyes soaked up each line she was held imprisoned, like water trapped in a sponge. She was totally captivated about the contemptible, but gallant message the poem held. When she finished reading the last line she looked up at him, with tears glistening of pure love in her eyes. In the soft light of the tent Thomas walked over and wiped her cheeks as tenderly as he would wipe tears from a dove. With the saline infused liquid lingering on his fingers, he looked not at her but, *into her*. They were now eye to eye, bound in a silk cocoon of the heart, wrapped inextricably by a mystery, and surrounded by the enigma of their love. Thomas and Heather were momentarily whisked away on the wings of mental and emotional bliss and conjoined by their spirits in a place that exposed the underlying current of their intense affection—they were in a different light, a different time.

Suddenly there was a call from outside the tent. "MAJ Michaels", the voice called out.

If either of them heard the voice there was no sign of it as they held each other in a trance-like gaze.

"Sir, are you in there?" The voice questioned as it moved closer.

Thomas seemed totally unaware that anyone was trying to get his attention, he was still held fast in the protective silk of the intertwining of his and Heather's very soul.

"Commander!" The voice bellowed once more.

It wasn't until the last of her tears had evaporated from his fingers did he respond.

"Yes, First Sergeant, what is it?" He questioned lethargically, and with more than a hint of agitation in his voice, as he moved to the front of the tent and stepped half outside just as 1SG Hillman reached the olive drab canvas flap which was a poor excuse for a door.

Half aware that he just might be disturbing Thomas, Hillman carefully said, "Don't mean to bother you sir. It's just that I thought we'd talk about doing a jump Tactical Operations Center (TOC) tonight."

"Night maneuvers?" Thomas thought. He quickly reckoned within himself, *"Something strange and wonderful is happening, I don't fully understand it but, I'm on the verge of discovery."*

The last thing Heather wanted was to move or jump the Tactical Operations Center in the middle of the night. It meant tearing down the entire campsite; all the tents, the mess section, the tables, the showers, their gear, everything, and loading it all on the vehicles, travel several kilometers and setting it all back up again—this could take hours. She watched Thomas as he stood half silhouetted in the doorway. Staying in the shadows of the tent, she casually, quietly, and deliberately moved within the shadows and over toward him, just out of sight of Hillman. She moved as if she had done this a thousand times with him, she reached out and tenderly took his hand, the way lovers do. The way you do when you truly care for someone.

"Top, a night move is out tonight. The troops had a long day with the range and all, and I myself have some reports I need to finish so I can have them dispatched to headquarters in the morning." His choice to be economical with the truth was effortless.

The moment she touched him he felt the warmth of her hand. He didn't jerk or make any sudden movements; it was as though he expected it. He felt the smoothness of her palm, and as their fingers interlaced he felt her familiar reserved strength, as she gave a little squeeze. The First Sergeant continued to speak in the dark from outside the tent.

"I guess we can do it another night. The men and women did alright at the range. I think the two new females will work out fine, they had some pretty good scores."

"Yes, I did look over the scores. The company as a whole did well. I was also glad that everyone fired. Tomorrow we will clean the weapons."

In the darkness the heat of their physical touch was growing. It began as Thomas returned her squeeze with an interlaced caress of his own. The silent power between them was making noise, the movement was slow, breathtaking, and amazing as the energy of their affection was felt through the touch of their fingers, and hands. It traveled up their forearms, and then snaked its way silently up their biceps, triceps and shoulders. The progress was pleasurable, tantalizing and effortless. It was now in their muscle, their blood, and all through their veins—it was every where. Thomas's and Heather's control was incredible. They remained poised, quiet, and above reproach as the invisible conductor within them instructed the orchestra of sensation to play a most stirring, synergetic filled symphony announcing to every part of their body that their love was vast and becoming unstoppable.

Hillman had no idea what was brewing just a few feet away from him and would have never believed it if he were privy to it.

"Just a quick note sir there might be some tension developing between Irving and Deville. I know what a *know* it all Deville can be, but I don't know much about Irving. Did she say much to you when she drove with you in the Hummer?"

"No. We didn't talk much." His decision to keep lying wasn't given a second thought. "I wouldn't put to much stock in anything Deville is mixed up in. She's seems to be jealous of every female in the company. Irving seems okay, even though I don't really know her."

"Well, I'll keep an eye on those two. We don't need any trouble out here. I just want to do these two weeks and get those kids trained and back to L.A. safely. Irving seems harmless enough." Hillman paused, then added, "She is a looker."

"Really?" Thomas questioned as if he never noticed anything about her. The chemical insurgents in his body was near its limit as a surge of its force struck out as Heather squeezed his hand tighter—this was a direct result of Hillmans comment and Thomas' retort—as it was the first signs that the power surging between them was reaching its breaking strain. "She's just another troop, looker or not, I'm just here to make sure she's trained."

Hillman began to speak about how he should find a girl, and settle down. Said he shouldn't be such a dreamer, so distant, and how he needed to loosen up.

"Top, I really have to finish those reports, and we both have to get some rest before tomorrow—our training schedule is full."

Hillman, understood, made a remark or two about the next days training and took his leave from his commander. Thomas watched as Hillman disappeared in the darkness.

The moment their conversation ended Heather had let go of his hand. She didn't want to let go, she had to let go, for if she had held on any longer she would have cried out as the orchestra within played the overture.

With a movement just natural to who he was, Thomas urbanely placed his entire body inside the tent and let the flap fall. "Sorry about that." He apologized, even though he knew she was well aware the blame wasn't his to bare. Thomas felt his heart suffer vertigo. He was now completely alone with a woman he knew, and yet didn't know how he knew her so well. He could read her thoughts, feelings, and desires. He was totally in tune to her in a way that defied logic, and entered into the mystic,.

"Your poem..." Heather began.

"I know." Thomas gently and kindly interrupted.

Heather smiled, it was her compliant smile. She knew full well that he knew how the poem had affected her, and now there would be no indirect communication, no more trying to reason the unreasonable. Thomas saw her in the half-light. She was lovely, feminine, and radiant. He took notice of her hair, face, arms, and legs. He was compelled by some unseen and unknown force to now physically act—yet he hesitated.

Heather, felt Thomas's eyes on her. She felt them take full measure of her hair, breasts, arms, and legs. She was extremely pleased that he liked what he saw. She was his, and had always been his. The inevitable had manifested itself. Destiny was being fulfilled they were now in their present—their light. Yet Heather heard his thoughts as he tried thwarting something decreed by fate years before they were consciously aware of each others presence.

"*Stop Thomas!*" He screamed at himself. Judiciously he continued to plead with himself and his very moral soul. "*Let this go! Let her walk out! Call Sergeant Hillman back and tell him the training is back on! Thomas you don't have to do this, not with her, not now!*" Logic and reason was losing to mystification, familiarity, and a love that was forged in a different time, in a different season. Before giving in, Thomas let out one last guttural cry to himself. "*This is insane, you must control this, leave! Call the red head at the office, Karen. Take her as you once did. Take her to the edge of heaven, enjoy all the pornographic delights she wields, but stop this now, you have the power.*" If he did have it, it wasn't evident, nor was it enough to stop what was going on between himself and Heather.

Thomas moved like a wraith in the shadows. Before Heather heard him speak he was standing in front of her with his hands in hers, bringing her to a standing position. What he said in the tent was prophesy, being fulfilled. With an understanding he was totally unaware that he possessed. Thomas tenderly squeezed Heather's hands as he looked deep into her eyes, all the way to her soul, and said, "You may not understand this, but you are my limit."

Heather immediately went weak in the knees. She understood it better than he knew, suddenly tears began to fall.

"These last few days you have made me profoundly happy because as my feelings are x and getting closer to that intangible thing called love, like y, I'm growing closer to a number and that number is you—my limit."

At this point there was nowhere to go but to each other. Reality had given way to romanticism and stars began to collide. They both knew without saying, that this was the way it always was between them; affectionate, doting, loving, and, adoring.

Tears still flowing, realizing she had finally come home, finally fulfilled her childhood dreams, she was finally reunited to her brother. She laid her head against his chest and instantly he hugged her, blanketing her in the darkness. As if on queue, the moonlight seemed to strategically shine through the tent, draping, covering and shimmering over Heather and Thomas. They began to glow. If they felt ill at ease there was no sign of it as Thomas gracefully slid his hands around Heathers waist, drawing her even closer.

Heather took in the fragrance of him, familiarly clean, manly, strong, loving, and inviting. A corporeal, and mentally alluring scent. It was an aroma that matched her body chemistry exactly, as though they were twins.

While Thomas and Heather emitted, and exuded in the moon enhanced light of true love, the woodland creature's normal night clamor seemed to form beautifully blended sounds that put a rhythmic beat to their burbles. Thomas and Heather slowly, unconsciously swayed in time to the tempo. As he led and she followed she could feel his body through his shirt, firm, smooth, and agile. He was the man of her dreams, in a lifetime of dreams where she never dreamed about a particular type of man. If this wasn't happening to her, she would and could never believe it. Just physically close, moving to and fro in the tent under the music and in the light of nature, they were dancing, romancing, fore playing on what was coming. She knew this had to be a dream, and if it was she didn't want to awake. Here she had been transported mentally, emotionally spiritually and now physically to a different plane of existence. A place she never knew existed. A place where she never knew she could feel this way—or think this way. Deep in the recesses of her mind she wondered how this man could make her experience this measure of completeness. The answer never came directly, but she knew it was wrapped up in who he was, what he experienced growing up, his creative aura, and the fact that he was a twin, and in the psychological-babble he would spill from time to time.

He once told her that the humans that populated the world were more into socializing, pleasing themselves, and always wanting to be amused or entertained, looking for an easier life, a better life. They rarely considered they were a part of the world, the universe. "We are all connected, everything and everybody." He had once told her life isn't about self gratification. Some know that, but many, far too many didn't, and the sad thing is they don't even think about it unless it's at Christmas time. Christmas is a great time but, what makes that holiday glorious; the celebration of life on earth—of happiness in this life—is the essence that should be celebrated *everyday.*"

Heather didn't know about the essence of life or why humans did what they did, or perceived things in the ways they did. What she did know now was after hearing Thomas's views she would never look at her own life perceptions the same. As for now, this night, she was totally vexed, and bewildered by this man—a man she knew so well, yet not at all. As they moved closer toward each other in the darkness, everything felt so right, yet she was so afraid. What surprised her the most was she wasn't afraid of Thomas, or herself, she was afraid of the situation—the unexplained ability of it all. This was no chance meeting, this was predestined and the answer was right there in front of her. She felt Thomas's chest against her face, and he felt her breasts against his midsection as they tenderly embraced. The maneuver was simple smooth and unassuming, yet it revealed and alleviated so much. She knew what was coming and wanted it, welcomed it, she was being completed in ways unexplainable. It was more of feeling, more of knowing—something akin to faith. She was together with him again, in the present—in the light. Today and yesterday seemed to have come full circle. Their memories had become the light. They weren't running away from anything, or running toward anything, they sort of just appeared together, after a pairing that neither of them could consciously recall. It was as if their souls had lived, loved, lost, and now rejoined their lost love. Completely uncanny, undoubtedly insane, yet it was happening and Thomas knew it as well. In the darkness the first kiss came like their whole relationship—expected, yet unexpected. It came like it always did—initiated simultaneously. As their lips touched an almost mystical clairvoyance of their emotional, mental, spiritual and physical self became completely aware of every crease, and crevasse of their carbon based existence. They were plunged head first in a tempest, a stormy season, in a place, in a time, in a world, within the great circle of the celestial sphere. There in that realm nothing existed except themselves as complete ethereal beings. They now began to thrive with a oneness that was filled with passion, enthusiasm, and the purest form of true love ever experienced by two human beings on this or any other planet. In the instant their lips touched the entire unknown was known, all the guesses became facts and all the denials, became reality. Heather and Thomas belonged together, were designed to be together in a way that is opaque to all others, but transparent to them. Their union existed before conception. Together as one then split into two, yet still together, they coexisted for nine months inside their mother's womb. Then birthed simultaneously due to a caesarian birth, and for six years they were together in the physical world. They were thick as thieves, closer than close, knew each others feelings, thoughts and could finish each other sentences. Then unexpectedly tragically their union abruptly ended. And since that day their spirits were trying to find their way back to one another. And now the journey was complete. Absolute in a way that defies all logic—just the way true love does. The way was made for their love to be fully experienced and not be kin. Heather was given life on the exact day and time Thomas's sister had died. In this season, in this place, in this time, in this world where nothing existed except themselves as complete ethereal beings, they knew all this they were able to comprehended the incomprehensible. They were the same, yet different, they had been together, yet parted, and most of all their love remained and because of a fatal accident a sister was no longer a sister— yet orchestrated to formulate, create, an entire different person—with the soul and spirit pattern of their love. They both knew they had become who they were supposed to be—for the very reason they were together now. It was time to rejoice, to celebrate on levels and in dimensions marvelous and dire. Thomas and Heather were coming home and moving away at the same time; the important thing was that they were doing it together.

That one kiss let loose an ocean of thoughts, memories, and knowledge which all flashed through their subconscious mind in an instant, but for them it was a lifetime. Thomas and Heather would mentally and consciously retain very little now, but over the course of the next thirty years would eventually recall it all. For now the kiss turned into more, so much more. The night skies turned even darker. The moonlight faded into nothingness as clouds covered its face and the rhythmic burbles of the animals ceased. It was dark, quiet and cozy inside the tent and Thomas and Heather were now caught in a mental, emotional, spiritual and physical, extraterrestrial upheaval, totally inebriated on the knowledge of their transfiguration. With their arms wrapped around each other and their lips pressed together ever so lovingly, they both felt the overwhelming, unmitigated, fervor of their love consuming them.

* * *

 Still partially nude in her backyard, Heather was riding the imaginary currents constructed at the time of an Equinox. Her mind held fast to that night, of that One Annual Training. The Santa Anna's were dying down and her air bath was coming to an end. Nonetheless the intensity of Thomas and the completeness she had as a woman on that night with him was still there no matter how hard over the years she tried to deny it, repel it, and eradicate it—the recollection of that entire event would and could never be removed. Endless tears of pain, longing, and loss flowed down her cheeks, and despite the calming winds, her tears never evaporated. The years since had not been emotionally, mentally, or spiritually kind to her. She had tried to maintain and pretend, but she could never fully suppress her, Thomas. And since her divorce from Bruce it was extremely difficult to actually deal with the knowledge of what she and Thomas shared that night so long ago. Heathers' waking days was a matter of acceptance, her sleeping nights—if you could call them that—were nights of denial.

 Thus in her minds eye, despite the three decades that had passed, Thomas to her was still the same in the way he looked, smelled, sounded, felt, and tasted that night. Heather closed her eyes once more, as the winds picked back up. As a wisp of air touched her nipples she shuddered and called to Thomas who was right there with her.

 She remembered how the cot in his tent seemed like a California King, with Egyptian cotton sheets and a goose down comforter. And ever so quietly, ever so gently, ever so tenderly they mystically floated down upon the bed. She never remembered them physically taking off their clothes. It was as if their garments dissolved instantaneously as their bodies touched the feathers. As there corporal shells merged upon one another, Heather could feel the strength of Thomas, it wasn't just in his tight abdominals, as their stomachs touched, or his firm chest as it pressed against her bare breasts. It wasn't just the strength of his arms and fingers as they caressed and held her back, buttocks, legs, and thighs. It was his inner, undefined, natural strength of someone who touches to please, to give, to provide pleasure not for oneself but for their partner. His movements were inspired, and made her entire being dazzle with every touch. A touch so tender, so gentle, like the invisible wind: tantalizing, mysterious, yet powerful and very pleasing. It was as

Memories, Light, & Promise

though he was an epicurean, and with his refined tastes and devotion to pleasure he was now enjoying the greatest feast he ever had the delight to experience and bestow.

The experience was so much more than his wonderful, excitingly, erotic physical touch. It was the fact that they were together in some cosmic celestial divide, not of this or any known world. It put the experience in a spiritual nebulous that made lovemaking in all it's over used, under warmed terms not even apply. They were bonded in another dimension, another time, enjoying and experiencing something that had no name, which had no meaning. Their kinship was not for mortals and it wasn't for Gods, it was a single attraction, like none other, designed for them and them alone. Yet it has been and will be longed for by many—forever.

Heather shuddered once more in the darkness the same way she did that annual training. It was an all encompassing realization that she wasn't—that she was dreaming. Heather knew that Thomas had utterly and completely possessed her, owned her, and she him. The surprising thing was that all her fear, wonder, amazement and apprehension were gone. It was as if this was how she was supposed to experience life, with a partner—effortless, guiltless, doing without trying—doing exceedingly well without trying.

The effervescence of their liberation of togetherness never truly ended nor died; the physical part seemed to have a beginning when they first kissed, but how long was she in that tent with him? How did she get back in her tent, and when did the morning come? She had awakened the next day to find herself in the tent alone, and the sun shinning brightly. This frightened her, for she had no recollection of ever leaving Thomas's tent and returning to hers. The last thing she could fully remember was the kiss she received from Thomas. Then being warped into another place, time, world, universe, and dimension. She felt completely satisfied in every area of her self, soul, essence, spirit, core, heart, body, nature, personality, and consciousness—how, why? There was something nagging at her mind, pulling, tugging her, promoting to make her remember, but she kept falling short. She thought of Thomas and instinctively touched herself between her legs—there was no soreness, a refreshing wetness, and a very faint—dreamlike pleasurable memory of whispers and kisses in the dark and Thomas inside her, taking her, over and over again. The heavy breathing, the panting, the desire and the will to be taken anywhere he wanted and arriving exactly where she wanted. Heather stood from her cot and sat back down. She rubbed her head and wondered did she dream all of the last evening. She had no conscious memory, a feel, an essence, and that was in drips and drabs. She longed to see Thomas. The very thought of him filled her with a joy that she couldn't describe. It was as if everything she ever wanted was given to her, and somehow for some reason Thomas made it all possible. The next thing she did surprised her completely. She went over to her foot locker knelt down and opened it and at the very bottom under a pile of uniforms she pulled out the poem. Like a satisfied virgin remembering her first time, a delightful little smile appeared upon her face. She mentally harkened back to several series, of long sequences of physical, mental, emotional and spiritual organisms. It was something she never ever knew existed or that the body, heart, mind or her psyche could accomplish. Then as she put the poem back something odd struck her in the deep recesses of her mind. She caught a flicker of Thomas looking deep, unblinking into her eyes, as they laid naked upon feathers in a place unknown, and he had said something to her that would never leave her, but would later make perfect sense.

"I know you love me just as much as I love you. I want to thank you. For a long time in ways I never understood, I've been trying to connect with something…someone, and that with me. And since I was six years old, somehow, I knew this moment would come. I have been endowed with a perception that defies all logic, but what is real, right here, right now, is you and I together, and I love you with all that I' am and all that I will ever be." Heather remembered seeing tears in his eyes as he said this and wondered how could she make this amazing superman of men cry? Yet it would be years before she fully realized the enormity, the complexity, and the revelations that were uncovered in the light of that night.

6
Light – Part 2

The next week and a half were like a blur. There was intense training during the mornings, the afternoons and the evening hours. Thomas and Heather saw each other but never seemed to get a moment alone. Each of them shared a sense of longing and it was growing stronger every day. They both wanted to give up the Army for the rest of the days of that annual training and spend the time with one another. This was conveyed through mental and emotional innuendo, insinuation, and nuances. Physically all they could do was make alluring eye contact that expressed their true desires. She was happy; she smiled all the time, a smile that was radiant, healthy and joyful, it spoke louder than any words.

This subtle yet unmistakable state of bliss wasn't perceived just by Thomas. SGT Deville did not and would never know the depths of Heather's and Thomas's affection, yet her natural envy and jealously seemed to heighten, thus giving her an acumen into these two that unbeknownst to Thomas and Heather was threatening everything. SGT Deville had been in the unit for two years. She had fallen in love with Thomas the moment she laid eyes on him.

Two nights before the end of the Annual Training Thomas and Heather finally received a moment alone. It was late, in the inky dark face of the sky you could see her dimples as the stars twinkled from the far off glow of the lamp light of the sun. The two stood close, hand in hand as they looked up and saw the constellation of Orion, the great hunter.

"That's strange." Heather quipped.

"What?" Thomas questioned looking skyward.

"That we are able to see Orion." Heather replied.

"Well, second to the Big Dipper in the Ursa Major, the constellation of Orion is one of the most recognizable patterns of stars in the northern sky." Thomas added.

"I know that, it's just that each constellation is visible for a range of months, depending on your latitude and its declination. In addition, the constellations rise and set like the sun and the planets so the time of night one is out stargazing matters when you would actually see them."

"So is this like some omen?" Thomas asked.

"Well Orion was a hunter. He had a warrior's heart. He was strong, brave, and still met a tragic end thanks to love."

Thomas looked puzzled. "I thought according to Greek mythology, Orion was in love with Metrope, one of the Seven Sisters who form the Pleiades, but Metrope would have nothing to do with him. Orion's tragic life ended when he stepped on Scorpius the scorpion. The gods felt sorry for him, so they put him and his dogs in the sky as constellation."

Heather smiled her you are right but not completely right smile. "Yes, but another version of the Orion myth says he was deeply in love with Metrope, Daughter of King Oenopion of Chios. Nonetheless, he was consistently denied marriage to her. Yet his love for her went on and on, and then one night in an inebriated state he raped Metrope. Metrope's father then consulted with Dionysis and found revenge. Dionysis cast Orion into a deep sleep and plagued him with blindness. Upon awakening Orion sought the help of an Oracle. It told him that to gain his sight back, he would need to travel east, and let the rays of the sun strike his eyes. Orion did this, regained his sight, and later lived in Crete, where the goddess of the moon Artemis fell in love with him. Her love for him was so strong, that she failed to light the evening sky with moonlight. Orion's death came about when Apollo challenged Artemis to hit a speck among the waters of the ocean, not knowing that

Memories, Light, & Promise

this speck was Orion swimming. Artemis shot a single arrow killing him. In response to her actions, Artemis placed Orion, along with his companions Canis Major, and Canis Minor in the sky, near the seven daughters of Oenopion, the Pleiades."

They both stood silent, for a very long time. The talk of constellations, Greek warriors, and Gods seemed familiar to them, and to talk about it was a joy. Yet they both were avoiding something…their own questions, about themselves. And now in full view of Orion, Thomas wondered, "Would he be able to maintain his love for his Metrope?"

He and Heather had so many questions, and so many answers. Some they knew and some they didn't. Some were asked and answered with just a thought, a look, or a caressing touch. They held an in-depth conversation without ever uttering a word. When the silence was finally broken it was Thomas who vocalized the words. They were words that had to be said aloud, and answered aloud. They were the words that inevitably had to be *spoken*. Thomas slowly turned to her and looked lovingly in her eyes and asked, "So, with us knowing what we know about each other, what are we going to do now?"

Heather wasn't in the least surprised by the question. It was more than expected, but expecting something and being able to deal with it once it arrives is two different things. Her reply was slow to come, honest and yet totally unrehearsed. She looked directly in his captivating blue eyes, noting that he now had tears that matched her own. Then mellifluously, yet with an uncanny gut-wrenching timbre, she found her self saying, "I honestly don't know."

The unclear atmosphere had nothing to do with the hour, but everything to do with the moment. Thomas didn't expect her reply, yet he had no answer to his question either. Like the Orion myth he knew his version, and needed to know hers or even if there was another version. With a little hesitation and in complete innocence he said, "I'll go back with you after this Annual Training. I could meet with Bruce and explain, just talk with him and tell him what we have discovered. I know it won't be the easiest thing to do, it even sounds crazy, but I'll get it done, I'll make him understand."

She smiled once more, and squeezed his hand tight. She was now full of emotions, and her tears flowed fully. Through a cracking voice full of love, and sincerity she said, "I am quite sure you could explain it all, but I am just as sure that Bruce would never understand it at all. You are making a mistake thinking that Bruce or most people for that matter think in these terms. People don't understand the supernatural, magic, passion, myths or any of the things you and I have shared in just these last two weeks. You talk or write about that and people will call it bull-shit! Thomas you are not of this earth. We stand together in the light of an unfathomable discovery. You are not from this season. Bruce isn't any better or any worse than you are. It's just that he has been too conditioned by the world to conceive anything but what he has learned. His entire life he has never had to feel or think on these levels. If you came and presented it to him it would be like having the tooth fairy, the Easter Bunny, and Santa Clause convince you that they are all real beings."

Feeling an incredible hurt well up inside him, and trying to use his Warriors heart to knock it down, Thomas retorted with humor as a defense mechanism. "You mean they aren't real?"

Heather laughed, and replied sweetly- maternally, paternalistically, the way a long time lover would. "Only to you dear. Only to you."

"Something has to give. We cannot lose what we have." Thomas said this with a whine in his voice.

"I agree with you darling." Heather said softly. She turned and put her arms around his waist and her head on his chest. In the darkness he hugged her as well. After a long hush, and an eerie calmness, she spoke, "You and I are one. You and I have, and continue to experience the unexplainable. Our minds are one. Our thoughts, feelings, emotions, and dreams have come together like nothing else. You and I possess each other in a way that defies all logic. When we are together we are not on this earth, this plane of existence. We meet somewhere in a phenomenon, where the sun crosses the equator and day and night everywhere are of equal length and within the great circle of the celestial sphere."

Reading her mind, knowing all that she has expressed was real, he finishes what she is about to say, "Equinox, it is there that we enjoy our memories and dwell in our light, and look to the promise that is us."

"Yes," Heather said, and she continued saying, "There is no you, no I, just..." In unison Heather and Thomas cried out..., *"us."*

"Yes my darling, us. If there were ever two souls, two spirits searching for one another they have found one another. We were one, split into two and now back as one. That night in your tent, I remember, that marvelous, interlacing of our souls and spirits. Destiny and love had taken a tangible form and melded us together as one." As these words were spoken they were once again engulfed by each others spiritual essence as a stillness settled over them.

Thomas pulled her close and began to speak with pure emotional zeal. "It's unmistakable, inarguable, and now inconceivable for us not to be together. You are no longer you. I am no longer me. We can no more go back to our lives than a butterfly can go back to being a caterpillar. It is you and I. I'm the one for you and you are the one for me. I know this, and you know it as well." Thomas' passion and fervor were alive and electrifying. He was talking from a truth, an unshakable position. It was alluring, wonderful, and very comforting. "We can do anything together. Go anywhere. Accomplish anything. Travel any path because we are the ones. We can now shape our own future on our own terms, and remaking the matrix, the fabric of destiny and our lives anyway we want to. The power is ours and it has been given to us through our strange wonderful love, which we now share throughout every fiber of our being."

"Thomas, please stop!" Heather cried out as she pulled away. She then covered her eyes, bent her head and slowly walked off in the darkness sobbing. Her gait took her about twenty paces, before she stopped and crumpled to the ground. Before she touched the grass and dirt, Thomas was right there by her side, and for a long moment she and Thomas sat on the earth, listening to the soft audible and inaudible cries of each other.

"Thomas, when we were alone in your tent and transported to that other world, I remember something. I don't remember everything but I do remember this... all of your power, your superhuman strength, your warriors' heart, and most all your unlimited potential. You posses a power unlike anyone of this earth. You are strong, kind, sensitive, giving, caring, tender, loving, intuitive, and everything anyone could ever wish for in a man—no in a human being. You are a poet, an artist and a warrior. That is who you are. You are even more than you know. I know this because I'm your other half. Yet for years I've compromised where you haven't, I have settled, and made choices that you haven't. And I envy you. You aren't looking to the horizon, or at the horizon." There was a pause, then she said, "Thomas you are the apparent juncture between earth and sky, something that is real yet not real at all. What I'm trying to say is that the difference between you and I is that I look to the stars, and you don't. I want to reach the stars and you don't, and the reason is because...You are the stars. I can't be the horizon. I can't be the stars." She looked up at Orion. "You don't belong down here with me. You really belong up there." Goose bumps appeared on their arms as an eerie coldness surrounded them. Heather's voice trembled and changed slightly as she tapped into and spoke from a place in her subconscious that was in a trance of its own, now channeling a power emitting from a place not of this world. She said, "Don't you understand! I know you, I am you, and I love you. I always have loved you, and looked out for you. I love you so much that I cannot and will not keep you tied to me on this earth. What happened to your sister all those years ago wasn't your fault, let go of the guilt. You have been searching for me all your life and you have found me. If this was a different time or a different place or if I had made different choices we could be. Maybe, and maybe, we would still have to come to this conclusion. At this time in my life and yours, our meeting is for me to let you know I'm here and I will not destroy the *praeter naturam* thing that is you."

Thomas was in tears. Heather had nailed it. She knew him, all the hidden thoughts, all the denial he put himself through for years, she explained. He felt he had to speak, but as he opened his mouth Heather silently and swiftly stopped him with a kiss.

Then she said, "Thomas, please let me finish this, because you know the excruciating pain it is causing me. You know that you are stronger than I am, stronger physically, mentally, emotionally, and spiritually. You have that power of persuasion, and I would be forced to look at things your way. What you say would be logical and sound, but... but I feel—no, I know I have a responsibility to you, to say the rest of this, and I will use your sensitivity, your feelings, and your respect for me, to do so. In the end whatever you decide I will do willingly, and with no regrets. I'll go wherever it is you ask." She paused, and moving close she began again, "I know I will never again achieve this level of consciousness, I won't have the romance, the stars and the Greek gods, the crystallomancy, the celestial planes of existence nor the most beautiful thing of all; our mind-melds. Your touch, taste, sight, sound, and smell, all the things you use so well to express your love to me, for me, and with me. You have given me the pleasure of mental, emotional, and physical organisms—love from a man who knows what a woman wants, what I want, and you can deliver consistently—on every level. But I have to forsake it because of choices I freely made years ago—the choice to marry Bruce and the choice to have a child. Walking away from that life would not be easy for any of them. I'd hate to consciously think what it would do to them if I did that. It is a choice I don't want to choose. I cannot imagine how he would continue especially in his line of work. The shame a scandal would cause would ruin his mental state, and then there are the effects all of this would have on our son. You see, I chose to be responsible and accountable and I always have been.

Yes, our love spirits have found each other, and by everything I hold dear, I love you. The Lord knows in my heart of hearts you and I belong with each other, to each other. In a way we are each other and have been before we physically met. Nonetheless, with all that said, I know where my responsibilities lie. You know me, and you can use that knowledge against me and you know I would have no choice but to listen and willingly obey you. Physically, mentally, emotionally, and spiritually, I cannot fight you—will not fight you, nor will I try. I want to stay in the light with you in the worst way. I *feel* all of you, and if you ask me to go with you and leave everything behind I would. Not to destroy the extraordinary thing that is you, but out of a purely selfish desire to experience all of you forever and ever. To have all my most inner desires fulfilled." Heather paused, wrapped her arms once more around Thomas, and cried, as she continued, "I want you to make me go with you and I don't want you to make me go with you. I don't have the strength on my own to make a firm decision, but you know me, better than I know myself. I have you and I have my responsibilities." She stopped and cried for a long moment, as Thomas held her lovingly. She looked up and in a voice so full of emotional grief she said, "I can't...I can't think anymore. I'm done you will have to do the thinking for both of us now." Right then she collapsed.

Thomas was now holding Heather and trembling mightily. He did know Heather Irving and he loved her more than life itself, and being a Major in the United States Military and the commander of one hundred and thirty soldiers, he knew a lot about responsibility and accountability. He was a leader and a great leader. He knew how decisions emotionally made would allow for culpability and guilt. He knew these things could transform people and make them act in ways that were contradictory to their nature and character. He knew the power he and Heather possessed over each other and he knew she was right in all that she had spoken. As he trembled he was fighting within his very existence. Fighting an impossible fight to slay the craving, the dependency, the cocaine that was her, that was now coursing through his entire being. She had laid an incredible burden, a Herculean labor at his feet—how do you give up the one you truly love? He was now crying with her.

They sat there shrouded by the blanket of the night and neither of them spoke a word for the next hour. Then out of no where and in a whisper, Thomas spoke, lyrically, prophetically, and truthfully. "What I am about to tell you, you already know, what I am about to say to you will never forget. What I am going to speak will never be spoken by me ever again to another human being. The truth is you are *my memories, my light, and my promise.* We are mated at the soul and spirit, and whatever we experience, mentally, emotionally, physically, or spiritually throughout all of our forms and levels of existence—what you and I have between us, cannot be shared by anyone but us. It can not be duplicated by anyone other than us, and will never die even after we die!"

And as if orchestrated, across the dark sky there was a loud thunder roll and a brilliant strike of lighting. In the next moment Heather and Thomas seemed to disappear from where they sat. Whether it was a great cloud formation blotting out every light in the sky, or some unexplained phenomena, for a brief moment in time Thomas and Heather were no where to be seen. They had once again slipped into that cosmic celestial divide. They were infused yet again in rapture, in another dimension, another time that was neither conscious nor unconscious, enjoying and experiencing their nameless passion. They were in the throws of a pleasure so erotic, so extraordinary, that it was clearly designed to be experienced for them and them alone.

7
Promise – Part 1

The next day Heather awakened in her tent unclear how she got there. She remembered whispers and touching in the dark, but how she left Thomas' side, arrived in her tent or if she had slept that night, it was all a mystery. She quickly dressed for the day and immediately stepped out of her tent into the hot sun. Subconsciously she noticed it was quiet around the campsite and for a second she felt alone. And to her surprise the first person she saw was Thomas—he was walking toward her. In her mind she heard Thomas say, *"You are my past, present and future."* She instinctively rubbed her forehead as if to get the fluids in her head flowing. *"It wasn't said like that."* She said to herself, *"It was more poetic; you are my memories, my light, and my promise."* Then she immediately remembered everything that followed. The thunder and lighting, the love making and how she made it back to her tent, missing the morning formation and being threatened by Deville.

"I know where you've been." Deville charged as her eyes glistened with jealously.

"I don't have time for this." Heather responded as she pushed past Deville and headed into the tent.

"You will have time when my father sends someone out to investigate your little romance with the commander!" Deville threatened with a jealous cry.

Heather was totally exhausted yet she paused, turned and looked directly into Deville's envious blue eyes. But before she spoke a single word it dawned on her that Deville was to be pitied, and prayed for. She now looked at Deville sadly and realized given another situation and another time she might have been just like her; An ordinary person who had been desensitized to anything out of the ordinary. A person who just stayed in her own world, and never really thought about anything on any different level than the everyday. Heather knew Deville was one of the millions that just went with the flow of life, and would always want but would never achieve, the true meaning and vibrancy of just being human. She would never know the exquisite and precious touches of the heart, nor have any knowledge of what was deep within the fabric of this existence. Deville and others were anesthetized by what uneducated, and over educated, friends, advertisers, false prophets, and people who were unable to see beyond their own problems, hatreds, and jealousies to know about the splendor of the human existence and its greatest gift, which was **love**. Deville's comment, *"little romance with the commander"* made Heather want to share the excruciating pain she was now baring. The colossal sacrifice she had to make and the agonizing choice she had to now live with for the rest of her life. Heather knew instinctively she would have to remain quiet about what she really felt. If there were any way she could explain the depth of what she and Thomas had discovered, she would have in a heart beat, but Heather knew that Deville was to cynical, too scornful and now too sarcastic, to be reasoned with or to listen. So Heather blinked back tears and took a hard honest look at Deville and said, "I am overjoyed not to be in your reality. I really am."

Deville was totally perplexed and stood there dumbfounded. Without another word being spoken Heather retreated to the tent and went to sleep in her cot. She fell into an unfathomable lyrical and eloquent sleep where she dreamed she was Psyche. The personification of the human soul from the the well-known fable of the Roman writer Apuleius. In her dream Thomas was Eros, the Greek god of love and sexual desire. She experienced how the goddess Aphrodite out of jealousy sent her son Eros to make Psyche fall in love with an ugly man. But Eros fell in love with the girl himself and visited her every night. Eros had forbade Psyche to see his face, thus she never knew what her lover looked like or who he was. One night she attempted to discover the identity of her lover. While Eros was asleep in her bed, she lit a lamp full of oil and bent over to see her beloved's face. Unfortuantly a drop of the oil fell on him and brought him out of his sleep. Eros knew she was trying to discover his identity and immediately left her and returned to the Gods. Psyche, heart broken and sorry for her act wandered the earth in search of her true love until she was finally reunited with him. They went up to the stars and lived happily ever after.

* * *

    This is where I physically joined the story and the episode began for me. I arrived mid-morning at Camp Pendleton. I began with an inquiry and after talking to MAJ Thomas, it was he who decided to recuse himself from the unit until the inquiry was concluded. My assignment to the case was highly irregular, but approved by my superiors, due to the nature of the case and the Inspector General, Colonel Deville, giving in to his whining daughter as she begged him to send someone out to investigate a case of fraternization in her unit of assignment. It was that afternoon when Thomas went to Heather and met her as she emerged from her tent.

* * *

    As Heather gazed upon Thomas she knew something was amiss he didn't look as he did in her dream. And when she saw me standing in the distance she realized Deville's father, the Inspector General, had sent me to conduct the investigation. Instantly she was reminded of her and Thomas' decision and how their life would never be the same again.
    Thomas approached and smiled uneasily trying to hide a sea of emotions. Heather smiled back, longing to submerge herself into his body. To her surprise, right there in the open Thomas tenderly took her in his arms putting them around her waist. He looked deeply in her eyes and saw his tears reflected in hers. He lovingly pressed his lips on her forehead and gave her a kiss.

She hugged him back and for the first time noticed the Humvee, it was packed with all his belongings, the foot locker he brought, his back pack, and his duffle bag. Superman was about to leave the planet. Her Eros was returning to the Gods.

"The end is nigh."

The adjective was appropriate, and its meaning clear, Heather thought. She knew this was what had to happen. After all they assimilated last night the time for words was over. She pulled back and now had streams of tears that matched Thomas'. She was smiling, but it was a smile of longing and loss. "Whenever you need me you know where I'll be." He whispered.

She nodded, as more tears welled up, and whispered back "In that great circle of the celestial sphere."

"It will be okay my darling. You know how to get there, if and when your responsibilities ebb." He paused then said, "In the meantime, if you just want to communicate, remember the time of the equinoxes."

"The vernal equinox occurs when the Sun crosses the celestial equator moving northward. The autumnal equinox occurs when the sun crosses the celestial equator moving southward." She whispered. There was silence, and in that moment of silence she glimpsed the twinkle between his tears, and noticed his last attempt. Though not spoken verbally, it was as loud and clear as if he was talking over a mega-phone. The look, the twinkle said, *"Think this over. We can still be together. We can leave together right now—fulfill the promise."*

Heather saw it, read it, and completely understood it, but she said nothing. She knew that she could leave with him right then. And if he had verbalized his desire, she would be compelled to leave with him. She felt herself go numb. She didn't want him to leave. She almost cried out and begged for him to take her.

Thomas knew she was fighting her own desires. He once again hugged her and this time they both were trembling. He was trembling with the knowledge of knowing he could resolve this, just by conversing with her husband, Bruce, and intelligently convince him why he should leave his wife. It wasn't arrogance, or some deviant wife sharing desire, it was that Thomas had that way about him, that when he knew something—he knew it, and no matter what anyone said to the contrary he could let you see it from his point of view.

But none of this was spoken. Thomas gently placed his hands on her shoulders and tenderly, lovingly kissed her once again on the forehead. In that one kiss he sent the message once more that they belonged together.

Heather said nothing, afraid she would say what her heart desired most—to leave with him. She felt his undeniable kiss of affirmation, and confirmation—they were one, always had been and always will be. And she knew that they would forever be each other's memories, each other's light, and each other's promise. She knew they were mated at the soul, and whatever they experienced, mentally, emotionally, physically, or spiritually throughout all of the forms of their existence—what they had between them would not, could not be shared by anyone but them. It would not be duplicated by anyone other than them, and would never die even after they died!

And it was in that moment the liquid sunshine began to fall. Some say it was just a freak rain storm that happens in the desert, but Thomas and Heather knew it was all of the heavens weeping at their inevitable departure. To me it looked as though Heather and Thomas had the water from the rain running down their faces. In retrospect I now know the water on their faces were tears, very heavy tears. Thomas and Heather were crying with the pain and agony felt by twins as they separated, one by life, one by death, an experience they suffered years ago which dealt out life and death in that instance.

The sky became very dark as the rain continued to fall. No more words were spoken between them and the normal noisy engine of the Hummer seemed quiet as thunder boomed and lightning flashed in the sky. The strange storm didn't last more than six minutes, by the time the rain stopped and the sun emerged once more. Thomas was gone. It was as though he didn't actually leave, but sort of disappeared in the darkness.

As the last of the darkness receded and the light returned Heather fell to her knees with her head buried deep in her hands, sobbing violently. She knew then that no matter what, unlike Eros's lover Psyche, she would not be roaming the earth trying in vain to find her lover.

* * *

The Annual Training ended the next day. The unit members were a buzz with the illicit affair and the absence of their commander. They behaved like most people who received half of the news—they made up whatever came to their minds. If you asked ten different soldiers what actually happened, you would get ten different answers and none of them were correct. Other unit members could care less and couldn't wait until they got back home to their friends, family and personal interests.

Once Heather arrived at the reserve Center she glanced around worriedly. She wanted to avoid going into the building. She could handle the ridicule, barbs, and condescending looks from her fellow soldiers, but she wanted to avoid seeing Thomas if he was there. She did know that if she saw him her heart would compel her to run to him and beg him to take her away. Her mind raced with visions of a new life.

To Heather's surprise her son Toby and I were there. Toby was ecstatic to see his mother, and he covered her in a thousand kisses. Being aware of the situation I smiled uneasily and said, "I'm glad you are finally home," as I kissed her slightly on the cheek. It was in that moment the rain began to fall ever so gently.

"Don't worry," I said, in a reassuring voice, "I'll get you home and we will talk everything over."

"Bruce I'm sorry I put you through this," Heather said tearfully and honestly.

Heather passed Norby and gave a little smile. Unexpectedly Norby walked up and gave Heather a supportive hug.

It was then a voice called from across the yard, "Sir, Major Irving, MAJ Bruce Irving, Sir " It was SFC Hillman. He was walking briskly as he called out. He reached us as we got to the car, nodded in Heathers direction and turned to me and asked, "Will you need to speak with any more of my people for your investigation?"

"No First Sergeant I have all the statements I need." First Sergeant Hillman saluted me even though I wasn't in uniform. I returned it. He thanked me and walked away.

* * *

Unknown to myself and Heather, Thomas was at the unit. He watched out from his office window as we entered the car. His eyes followed us as we drove up to the security fence. We were behind two other cars and inched slowly through as the guard raised the red and white crossing-arm. The liquid sunshine came down heavier and the skies darkened prompting me to switch on my headlights and wiper's.

Thomas stared in our direction as though he could actually see Heather. Heather must have felt his gaze, emotions, or something, because even though she couldn't see him she fidgeted and glanced around nervously.

"You alright Heather?" I asked.

"Yes, Bruce, I'm just tired." She said knowing this was a half-truth. "I'm just embarrassed at this whole thing and the spot this will put our marriage in."

"We won't discus this in front of Toby, but we will sort it all out." She squeezed my hand gently and I gave a little squeeze in return.

Heather was tired. Tired of not being able to see Thomas one final time, but in the car at that moment she did feel something, but she didn't want to risk seeing him.

Thomas was looking through the rain drenched window, and a single thought crossed his mind. *"Go out there and get her."* He could just break down in front of Bruce and Toby and beg Heather to go with him.

Heather turned once more uncomfortably in the passenger's seat. She somehow knew he was around.

Thomas knew he shouldn't have been at the center, but was compelled to maybe get a glimpse of Heather. In the intervening days since he drove his Humvee away from Camp Pendleton he terribly miscalculated his feelings for her.

Heather looked out of the window staring in the direction of the commander's office. Even though she couldn't possibly see in, she *knew* he was there. It was when she saw me and Toby waiting after she arrived at the center that the full immeasurable weight of her feelings for Thomas crashed upon her. What she subconsciously knew out in Camp Pendleton finally made its way to her conscious mind. She now understood what Thomas realized days ago, that they *belonged* together. But with her hand firmly grasped inside of mine and Toby playing affectionately with her hair, she was petrified by the visual reminder of her responsibilities.

Thomas stared out the window, unmoving as though he was in some hypnotic trance. His entire persona was focused on Heather. He sat like that for ten entire minuets with his eyes flowing endless cups of tears.

And for an instant Thomas and Heather did see each other, it was weird, wonderful, and mystifyingly incomprehensible. They didn't see each other physically, but their spirits met. The arms, torso, legs, hands, fingers, toes of their spiritual self flexed their celestial sinew, and psychically they touched.

And it was in that moment that Thomas from his office, and Heather from the car simultaneously in a whisper uttered, "*You are my memories, my light, and my promise. We are mated at the soul, and whatever we experience mentally, emotionally, physically, or spiritually throughout all of our forms of existence—what you and I have between us, cannot be shared by anyone but us. It will not be duplicated by anyone other than us, and will never die even after we die!*"

Their souls mated, they reached out, and they kissed.

Instantly, Thomas blacked out at his desk...

Heather fainted in the car...

I was turning making a right turn out of the gate and saw Heather collapse...I shook violently. I immediately pulled the car over, "Heather...darling," I cried. "Are you okay?" Her hand was ice cold to the touch and all the color was gone from her face. But, before a full panic attack set in on my part, Heather seemed to recover. "What's wrong with you Heather?" I questioned with a voice full of alarm.

"Is Mommy okay Daddy?" Toby questioned more than a little frightened by the ordeal.

In tears, Heather slowly regained her composure saying, "You both have to excuse me. I must be more tired than I know." She cried quietly as the liquid sunshine fell and I drove on.

8
Promise – Part 2

Sixty-Two equinoxes had past since that day and Heather never lost her connection with Thomas. In fact it grew. It was the strongest for some reason during the time of an Equinox. I never fully understood how, but I do know by the sheer power of their love, they were given some ethereal key comprised of a force that allowed them to channel their love and manifest an essence of a connection where they came together at that strange time of year. I used to watch as Heather would go into a subconscious trance and ride the uncanny currents that compose the celestial equator. "Are you alright?" I'd ask her and she would look at me and weep.

"Bruce I don't know, I just need a moment, please." She'd respond.

And for the next thirty minuets she would sit alone crying non-stop.

"I'm sorry. Please forgive me." Heather would say each time. It took me six years to realize these attacks came twice a year, in March and September. Then it took fourteen more years to realize at the moment when this happened, she was actually with Thomas. Ten years after that we divorced. That's when Heather's visits with Thomas were moved to the backyard. She sat for hours partially nude, and seemed intoxicated, as she reclined on one of the lawn chairs. From what I gather, the air bath was as close as she could come to remembering Thomas's touch.

The years brought great understanding for me. I first wanted her to talk to someone, a counselor or a psychiatrist, but this was all to no avail. I watched in vain as Heather struggled mightily to consciously deny her love for Thomas. Nonetheless, the intensity of Thomas and the completeness she had as a woman in those two weeks with him was still there no matter how hard over the years she tried to deny it, repel it, and eradicate it. The recollection of that entire event would and could never be removed. She loyally served and loved me and Toby and gave us her all, but a piece of her was gone. A piece I could never get back or reach. Together over the years she and I tried to reject, discourage and eliminate the entire event. But it would not and could not be removed. Heather suffered knowingly with me and there was nothing I could do because I just didn't have that connection.

I admire her still. Through our entire marriage she never tried to track him down or physically contact him, neither through letters, e-mail or by phone.

It took me a long time after the investigation to fully realize what happened between them during that Annual Training, and even now I struggle with it. Heather immediately gave up her career in the military after the investigation in which she cooperated fully. Her testimony and sworn statement were a mystery to me for years. She admitted she and Thomas were together but it was not a pre-calculated decision, nor was it out of lust. She could not fully explain their connection or why it happened. Her memory of the event was as if she was telling it as a bystander, and not an actual participant. She had no real conscious memory of the episode just the essence of what took place. But she took full responsibility for her actions.

I did forgive her for Toby's sake and for the love I held for her.

There is so still much I don't know about my wife and the relationship she had with Thomas Michaels. We agreed to never speak about it and just go on with our lives. We divorced a year ago, not long after our son Toby graduated from medical school, and got married. This was thirty one years after that One Annual Training. The episode always bothered me but, I didn't become totally obsessed with the whole thing nor have my dreams haunted until one day I stumbled upon this letter written from Heather to Thomas a few months after our divorce. That was when I opened Pandora's box;

> Dear Thomas,
> You and I both know our relationship will never truly be over and I hope you remember what we had. As I sit in the gentle breeze I realize, without you, my life has taken on a muted tone. No music, no color, no laughter... I find nothing in life entertaining. I don't like feeling like this and I plead with myself not to hold onto the past. I pray you don't forget our One Annual Training / you were my one true Superman.
> Our romance lasted two weeks but in reality, that bite into the Apple tasted like forever. Things ended way too soon between us and I thought I could handle it through the years. I thought gradually over time I wouldn't feel this way and hopefully one day I wouldn't think about you. I admit, I don't blame you because it wasn't either of our fault. Timing and responsibility is where the blame truly lies, but regardless of all of that ...I can't stop my eyes from tearing up. It's painful for me to think of the last time I heard you say 'I love you.'
> I should just let this die. We said our goodbyes, the details of that were uneasy then and at this point the details don't really matter. We both understood the price we were paying, and as I think it through I continually wipe away the tears. I wish this didn't have to be. I think about you way too often, things I see, hear, taste, touch and imagine always bring you to the forefront of my mind. I am usually distracted by thoughts of you. Bruce, Toby, friends and acquaintances ask me what's going on, why am I so distracted, and I cooly lie, and tell them everything is fine. I play it off and get back to reality but subconsciously I know our departure was a very big deal, and the truth is, I am not over you—nowhere close, I haven't moved on.
> I want and need you here. I'd like to confide in you, it would be great to see you again. I remember our time together as though it was yesterday. Our uncanny bond, auspicious beginning, our speaking without talking, the dark nights and the deep thoughts. I wonder now, do you do the same; pretend everything is fine when you think of me? Do you want to reach out to me as much as I want to reach out to you? I want to know if you just let the thought of me go and mentally walk away when you remember us, the stars, the Greek gods. I am not too proud nor in too much denial to confess that what we had

> was bigger than anything. Together we were physically, mentally, emotionally and spiritually bonded like no one else.
>
> You must remember those nights when we met in that celestial plane of existence, naked on all our levels of life. A place where we were transported and made love and cuddled on blissful nights that seemed to never end. You said it so hauntingly beautiful when you told me, I was your <u>memories,</u> your <u>light</u> and your <u>promise</u>—and for that I will always love you. I continue with Bruce and he is a very good man, and he is a great husband, but in the end he just isn't you. I hate you Thomas, and God knows I love you to dammed much. Your words echo in my head even now, "Our love was authentic and it will continue for as long as we live."
>
> The truth be told, when it's for real, its forever. Galvanized by all our nights, waking up still inside each others arms, minds, and hearts. I still want you in the dark, I need you in the light… I hunger for the equinox. I know you know from our experience that nothing can or ever will compare to what we have—this was yours and mine…first real and true love. You know despite other lovers you may have or may have had, our relationship was special and loving. We were kindred, we will never have anything like what we had again, because of our uncanny connection, we did more than understand each other and have fun. We were brothers, and sister's, best friends and lovers, the perfect match, soul-mates, we actually glowed when we were together that One Annual Training.
>
> I made the correct choice at the time, and you know it. I would have done anything for you, but harm Bruce and Toby—they were my responsibility. But I want another chance. I want to mend our lifelong bond. I don't want anymore "what ifs" between us. You see Thomas; I finally remember…our love has always been there. In the beginning before birth there was us—you and me. Though separated by family relations, death, responsibility, time, and going our separate ways our LOVE is still there. And that is because we are mated at the spirit. We did find each other and we received accommodation from the heavens. Thomas the thing is, and there is no way around it, no matter what, we cannot deny what happened out there between us. It's not just the heat of the flames of our love, but the fire, the passion that has illuminated and shown me that we belong together.

I could tell she worked hard at trying to put the pieces together and tried to fully understand what happened. I believe the reason she never tried to contact him during our marriage was three-fold. She was

Memories, Light, & Promise

trying so hard to be a good wife and mother, and she knew if she had contacted him he would probably come to her and she would let him. After reading that letter I can imagine the strength it took to not make contact, like dancing in fire and not getting scorched. In my dreams at night I'd toss and turn and have this vanity-guilt complex overcome me.

"Why wasn't I good enough for her? Was it the sex? Did he look better?" I fought my torrential emotional and mental anguish with binge drinking, until me and Jack had to take it easy. I went to see a therapist, Dr. Bridgette McGill. She was a very intelligent woman, with hazel-green eyes, and natural curly highlighted blonde hair. I remember her so well because not only was she easy going and could get along well with others, she gave me the best advice. "What you need to do Bruce is write everything down, everything you feel and think." I dated her after the divorce and she tried to help me get over Heather, but in the end I couldn't commit due to an ever nagging, and haunting internal guilt. I knew then I could never fully put this case behind me. I couldn't do it until I knew what had become of Thomas Michaels.

He was found guilty after the investigation and resigned his commission and never had anything to do with the Army again. I learned he became a full partner at his ad agency then retired some years later. He also published a book of portraits and poems. From his picture on the back cover I saw how he aged gracefully. He was still a strikingly handsome man, with eyes just as steel blue the day he met Heather. He still possessed a faded athletic figure, not as lean and muscular as he used to be but okay. His hair was silver and the lines that made their way around his eyes seemed to be airbrushed out. He had a slight sag of skin around his neck. I stared at this picture for over two hours almost against my will. I imagined all sorts of things I consciously never knew I thought about. Things like how Heather viewed this man; his thoughts, his politics, his body. Did she make love to me and think of him? I read the poems in the book and studied all his pictures. His artistic ability was incredible, the way he captured the light and essence of landscape and the mood of the poems were extraordinary. One poem in particular captured my attention and I knew he loved Heather to the point of death. The poem itself indiscreetly mentioned Heather's name, and if anyone had studied their relationship they would have known it was meant for Heather Irving herself. The poem was entitled **The Final Hour.** When I first read it, I saw the name and its reference, and saw how it fit into the rhythm of what was being said. It was after reading it several times that it hit me.

"Sweet Jesus," I exclaimed. He skillfully put that in there to tell Heather how he needed her. *"Did Heather know?"* I thought. It made me think more seriously about the poem **Bite into the Apple.** I went and got a copy from the file. I secretly kept the file of all the items from the investigation. I know Heater kept the originals and try as I might over the years I could never find them. It really didn't matter because after reading **Bite into the Apple**, with new found eyes, I appreciated its ingenious, yet subtly veiled adulterous implications. I then went and spoke to anyone who ever knew him. I spoke to dozens of people about him over six months almost everyday. To my chagrin, I began to really like the man. The sense I got from him was that he was a straight shooter, likable, down to earth. He was more than a renaissance man. Everyone described him differently but the same. It was as though he could tune into whoever he was with and befriend them. Immediately making them feel safe at their level. The most puzzling thing about what I learned of him was that after the episode during that Annual Training, Thomas Michaels never again was in a relationship with another woman. He had lots of admirers but it was like he had no inclination to be with anyone. Actually several of his business partners had said, *"They always liked Thomas, but after that thing with the Army, he sort of changed. He didn't talk much about his life before that and after that he never said a word. It was creepy; He came in, did his work but pretty much kept to himself. Some of us thought that he was real depressed."*

The most tragic thing I learned was that as he aged he was suffering from chest pain and was diagnosed having angina pectoris. It was a symptom of a condition called myocardial ischemia, which occurs when the heart muscle (myocardium) doesn't get as much blood (hence as much oxygen) as it needs for a given level of work. I did some research and found out that Angina pectoris can occur when blood circulation to the heart is sufficient for normal needs but inadequate when the heart's needs increase, such as during physical exertion or emotional excitement. Running to catch a bus, for example, could trigger an attack of angina while walking to a bus stop might not. I thought about the poem; **The Final Hour** again, and wondered if I should physically go find Thomas Michaels. After months of deliberation I retrieved his address from his file and found out he was still living in Santa Monica, CA. He had a Hospice nurse attending to him. I didn't want to excite him by my visit so I planned a visit the day she was there. I was hoping by visiting Thomas Michaels I could bring the whole thing to some sort of closure for myself.

What happened during my visit not only took me by total surprise but something that haunts my dreams still. Little did I know that the day I went to visit Thomas, it was the same day Heather had read Thomas' book of pictures and poems. It was then, after reading the hauntingly beautiful **Final Hour**, she knew she had to get to him.

* * *

Heather, was nervous, she hadn't physically seen nor spoken to Thomas Michael's since the findings during the investigation. She was a little surprised when she learned that, after all these years Thomas still owned and lived in the luxurious two bedroom townhouse less than a half a block from the beach in beautiful Santa Monica, CA. It was after she read his poem, **Final Hour** that she knew the time had come.

She read the poem by accident on the internet. Toby had given her a computer for her fifty-eighth birthday and over the years she became savvy enough with it to where she knew how to upgrade all the software and hardware. She did all her banking, and managed her investments online. On occasion she would surf the net. It was a year after her divorce she decided to *Google Search*; Thomas Michaels. In the back of her mind she wanted another chance as well. She had even written a letter a few months after her divorce referencing how she missed him and her intentions. She never mailed it and thought she may have miss placed it. She looked for it from time to time, but assumed it either was thrown out or mixed up in the items Bruce seemed to take forever to pick up, during the first nine months of their divorce.

Even before she typed his name in the search block and pressed enter her heart raced like a jet engine.

"*Calm down,*" she told herself as she saw a list of possible matches. She hesitated a moment then clicked on the first web link. She felt herself getting excited once she began reading the information on the page. There was a copy of his book just published and a link to one of his poems for sample reading;

Final Hour

My Warriors Heart made it impossible to convey
Most of me died in that, our final hour.
Life has closed in on me ever since that day
I wish I had found the knowledge to make you stay
Now the mythology of love has me trapped in its power

Never should I have let my soul-angel slip away
Year after Year the pain I feel is more than I can bear
Crying for relief I let a cowards escape enter the fray
My last thought is I wish today was our yesterday
Time, self pity and grief has made things unclear

I feel like the moor, dry without Heather
Yes, I hurt but I can't keep waiting at this celestial sphere
Breathing my last won't stop me from missing you forever
I pray for strength not to give Satan's woo any pleasure
Our hearts are calling and our love will free me from here

My Warriors Heart now made it possible to convey
I want to live and reverse this, our final hour
Life will open as I have faith that our hearts will join one day
Biting the Apple has given me knowledge to make you stay
Because of you the mythology of love will release me from its power

---

Heather read the poem and cried. She felt his loneliness, his longing and his depression. She could tell he was upset with himself, and for failing to act. Heather knew time had muddled things for him. He needed her and she needed him. It was their contact that would balance the scales and complete their lives. There was still time. Their chronological age here on earth had nothing to do with their timeless love, which had already survived so much. The poem did change its tone and perspective in the end. The emotion *"pod"* opened as he prayed to his redeemer to give him strength against Satan's Woo. And Heather saw how cleverly he had specifically mentioned her by name, and how their meeting at their imaginary place was no longer practical. She knew she had to get to him. The fact that this poem out of the twenty four that were in the book would be the sample, and for her to be reading it on the 20th of March—the signs were unmistakable.

She had to get to Thomas today. It took her ten minuets to pull up Thomas' last known address in Santa Monica, CA. The phone number was unlisted and she knew she could make the trip in just under an hour from Thousand Oaks. Within twenty minuets she was speeding down the freeway in a late model black Mercedes. She consciously floated in a sea of memories and emotions. Thoughts and feelings she forbade herself to feel unless it was during the time of equinox.

"Oh my God, I missed him so!" Heather began to cry as she always did when she thought of the emptiness, and painful routine her life had to take, and the same she had thrust upon him. She knew more now, she could explain the unexplainable. How their love was more of a test of heavenly and galactic proportions, more than a test of time. He was familiar to her the moment she was in his presence, but before that also. He was familiar to her before her birth, and during the life of his twin sister, she was the twin but not the twin.

Heather's tears came faster now as she deftly moved her car down the 405 freeway. She was moving once again now as the value x approaching her number and Thomas was y. She new she didn't have to reach her number because things were now in motion to pass through a whole or a discontinuity as herself the value x, because she moved closer to y, which was Thomas. She would be him, he would be her and they would reach their number, their limit, their LOVE.

They were together long ago before their mother's cell split into two. She was finally realizing their love was alive eons before their corporal bodies even materialized. Heather's breath caught in her throat, as the magnitude of what she and Thomas had weighted her conscious thought. She glanced over at the documents she had placed on the passenger's seat. There she had the poem *Bite into the Apple*. It was well protected, even though since the divorce she had handled it quite a lot in acid free plastic document protectors.

Heather's heart began to skip a beat when she drove up to his address. She sat in her car nervously for only a fraction of a second. Heather exited and walked up to his end unit and knocked anxiously on the door.

Her heart nearly stopped when the door slowly opened. A young blonde haired woman who looked about thirty stood in the doorway. "May I help you?" she said in a soft polite voice.

Heather was surprised and lost her voice momentarily. "I'm here to see Thomas Michaels?" she finally managed.

"May I ask who you are?" The women enquired.

"I'm Heather. Heather Irving."

"Oh my Lord!" The woman exclaimed as her face turned beet red as she became flushed. "I..I..am Misty." As she said this she stumbled backward and widened the door. "Mr. Michaels' has been talking about you non-stop the past few weeks."

"Who are you?" Heather questioned.

"I'm a Hospice nurse, and I've been assigned to Mr. Michaels."

Heather took a step back and held her hand to her chest as if she was having a heart attack. "Is he dying?" Heather screamed in a whisper.

"No. He recently had a couple of coronary artery spasms and I come here three times a week to monitor him."

"I need to see him!" Heather demanded.

"Darling I'm right here." Thomas' voice carried across the living room.

The moment was magical. Heather turned and saw Thomas standing there alive and in living color. He was maybe an inch or two shorter, and his hair was completely silver. His black knit polo shirt clung to what was left of his muscular body. His face now showed his age and worry lines had invaded the corner of his eyes and forehead. He looked as though he was a man waiting for something before he died.

As Heather and Thomas looked at each other a multitude of tears began to flow between them; tears of pure joy, tears of lost time, tears of longing, tears of happiness, tears of pain, and tears of love.

They embraced each other tightly yet tenderly. Passion erupted from them like ash from a long dormant volcano. The rapid eruption of emotions sent their hearts pounding and expanded into cardiac arrest. Their unbridled passion consumed them and seemed to fragment and obliterate blood vessels and arteries within their bodies. As they once again physically held each other, it was the final affirmation that they belonged together.

"Heather I love you so much," Thomas began in an aged baritone voice. "The strange and wonderful experience we had during that One Annual Training has never left me."

"You know I didn't want to leave you," Heather responded through a voice of tears.

"There is no need to apologize," Thomas said, "I should have held on tight to you and never let you go."

Heather kissed him hard and long, then said, "It was me I did nothing. I was foolish and stupid."

"No darling, we were both lying to ourselves." Thomas said as he squeezed her tighter.

"I was in denial for so long." Heather commented through a sob.

"All that's over my love," Thomas told her through a kiss, "We will never have to think about being without each other and our love again."

They continued to kiss passionately. "Over the years the yearning for our spirits to be together has grown." Heather added. "I will never leave you Thomas, I don't want either of us sitting alone. Back then I didn't know me, I didn't know you, yet when I made my decision I thought I knew everything."

"I know." Thomas responded understanding. "I learned a lot about myself, you, and us when we were together."

"It was so new and overwhelming and utterly unbelievable." Heather said as she touched his face and looked him in his steel blue eyes. "I had never felt the feelings you released in me and they are the same I'm feeling now."

"I love you." Thomas said, looking in her hazel eyes. "Now that I see your face, and hear your voice, kiss your lips, I know this is where we belong, right by each others side."

"Yes my love." Heather moaned passionately as she felt Thomas' kiss once more. "We do belong together. When we parted I lost a huge part of myself, a part I didn't know existed until I met you."

"We are mated in soul and spirit." Thomas spoke as he ran his fingers lovingly through her hair. "We had returned to each other then and now again. No matter how much I missed you, I knew we'd come back together."

"You always were my superman." Heather said as their spirits began their invisible journey through their bodies. "From the first moment I saw you, I felt I had known you. It was our souls, our spirits, our love that was finding each other here on earth. Even though I had my husband and son, I never felt as connected as when we were together. The things we shared late into the night, the speaking without speaking. I never met anyone kinder, smarter, lovelier, on so many levels. I know we are kindred and deep within our tripartite existence we know what we have will always be forever."

* * *

This is the moment I arrived and noticed Heather and Thomas holding each other tight and feverishly kissing and talking as though this was the first time and last time they'd ever be in this place together. If they knew I arrived I would never know it.

* * *

"Over time I became so depressed." Thomas cried. "I couldn't sleep at night or during the day. You were always on my mind." Thomas wiped tears back, "I need you to forgive me, I became so depressed I contemplated suicide."

"I know." Heather said understandingly, "I read your poem; **The Final Hour**. And I know you didn't give in to Satan's woo," Heather smiled, as she said that last line.

Thomas didn't seem surprised that she read the poem, and now knew she understood that it was his love for her that helped stay his hand. "I never listened to the radio, watched television, or went to the movies, because I was trying to take away anything that would stop me from thinking about you. I was so lonely."

"I know what you mean my dear Thomas." Heather said. "I had many days where I'd try to put you out of my mind and keep it together, but inside, I would be falling apart. I'd get a way from everything and just start to cry. I couldn't wait until our spirits met at equinox in the celestial sphere."

Their eyes locked affectionately, and through their glistening tears they gazed deep into each others spirit and made one final connection.

Thomas looking deeply, unblinking into her eyes, said his final words here on earth. "I know you love me just as much as I love you. I want to thank you. For a long time in ways I never understood, I've been trying to connect with something…someone and that with me. And since I was six years old somehow I knew this moment would come. I have been endowed with a perception that defies all logic, but what's real, is us, right here, right now— you and I together. I love you with all that I am and all that I will ever be."

The words were familiar it was what he had said to her so many years ago that first night he took her in his arms. Heather then fully realized the enormity, the complexity, and the revelations that were uncovered that Annual Training. Heather never spoke another word, just nodded approvingly.

It was in that very moment, the explosivity of their reunion had joyous and unexpected consequences. Everything their flesh, emotions, mind, and spirit experienced and enjoyed from that fateful Annual Training rushed through them like a runaway locomotive. This time it rammed through their natural bodies as their organs exploded from within, everything they saw, heard, touched, smelled, and tasted evaporated in an instant. It over took their souls. The energy interface was too much. It dissolved their mind, will and every emotion. It didn't cease until Heather's and Thomas' spirit stopped their hearts and left their bodies.

Misty and I watched in slow motion and horror as their intertwined bodies seem to float to the floor. What we didn't see but somehow sensed on a level of comprehension that frightens me to this very day was Thomas and Heather's ethereal form ever so softly, ever so smoothly, ever so lovingly, ghost-like hovering over their fallen mass. What we saw rise was like a white vaporous puff. I sensed that neither of them felt anything as their corporal shells merged, then their spirits. They were once again transported to the heavens, somewhere that mere humans can never travel. They were back together in some cosmic celestial divide not of this or any known world. They were once again experiencing each other in a spiritual nebulous that made lovemaking in all it's over used, under warmed terms, not even apply. They were in that other dimension, that other time, enjoying and experiencing something that had no name, which had no meaning. Their kinship was not for mortals and it wasn't for Gods, it was a single attraction, like none other, designed for them and them alone. They were now *love* itself.

The End

Debarkation

Through all of my Jack Daniel's induced, undistinguished purple-prose, I hope I was able to convey a compelling story: One that illustrates that Heather and Thomas were each others past, present and future, or as Thomas put it; memories, light and promise.

MAJ Michaels and Heather, Heather Irving, did reside in a different season and if I never believed it, seeing them die that way was truly convincing. The medical examiner ruled the official cause of death, for both of them as a heart attack. I know their attack of the heart was purely emotional and spiritual, and something that could not be contained physically.

I have a confession to make. All this time as I sat in front of my computer, with all my notes and paper work, I haven't typed a thing. The pain I feel hasn't been anesthetized by the alcohol. I struggle often to get it all down on paper, to get it out, so I wouldn't have to keep reliving this episode, this strange case that involved my wife.

As I stated before I embarked down this memory lane, it was near impossible for me to make the shift over to their different season. As you have deduced, the shift was extremely difficult for me because the events involving MAJ Michaels and Heather, Heather Irving asked me to forget that through all these years I am *still* in love with her.

When I first investigated this case I had to force myself to departmentalize my feelings. What happens now when I sit and try to write the story, I drink because this is tremendously demanding. The episode did happen and it wasn't until I researched Thomas's background and read Heather's diary's did I change my own self-fulfilling ideologies of right, wrong, decency, and what is and isn't sensible. Their death was the final piece I needed to fully understand their adulation, passion, and love. It transformed me from jealous, angry, and misguided husband, to realizing there are forces out in the world greater than what I learned from the media and university scholars.

There is so much I know and there is so much I don't know…but through the pain, and experience of this episode, I no longer mock or hold true love in contempt. I have realized what is attainable from the true alliance of one heart to another. And like I said before, I wish that it hadn't taken Heather and Thomas to instruct me in the ways of love. I want to write it but, I can never get past the pain. Nonetheless, I need to do something because if someone else could hear or read or see what I have experienced then maybe just maybe, it will make a difference in their lives, and they won't have to go through what I have.

I really did come to like and even envy Thomas Michaels. My obsession to learn everything about him was strange but needed in order for me to make an unbiased, and an objective opinion about him. After looking back on the entire ordeal over the past thirty plus years—questions still remain; Did Heather and Thomas find the intangible? Did the intangible find them, or was it always there? I do think that there are love spirits floating around, looking for each other. I know all this sounds crazy, but now the Jack Daniels I have been sipping on all night is gone and I'm truly inebriated. The alcohol makes it easy to deal with the entirety of it all. The facts are clear though; Heather was conceived the exact moment, that Thomas's sister died. And although Thomas never knew it, from that moment something inside of him was looking for her—not physically but spiritually.

I won't be writing the story today. The computer screen stares back at me with the cursor blinking impatiently, beckoning me to type something…But I can't. I know I have to stop being so weak, and stop revisiting this episode. The hope I was looking for needs to come from within. I need to balance what happened, emotionally and logically. I now place all the items back in the file. I pause as I touch the poems. There is so much depth in them. I read them once more. When I am finished, I rubber band the folder and stick it back in the drawer.

I will do the mature thing. The one person I will tell this story to is our son, Toby. I'll talk to him about his mother, Thomas and their love. There are some things about Thomas he really needs to know. Maybe just maybe, he can find what Heather and Thomas discovered in that different season. My wish for Toby and his wife is to be each others *memories, light and promise.* I know Heather cared about me and Toby with all of her heart, but she knew another love even before she met me and before she was born. I realize the incredible emotional turmoil she and Thomas must have suffered, because I suffer now. I too love Heather—it isn't on the level of hers and Thomas's. But it has allowed me to reflect on my life. And without becoming sickeningly sentimental; I am actually glad that I had this experience. It has taken years, but finally I have learned; that true love bears all things, believes all things, hopes all things, and endures all things. Most of all, love never fails.

Printed in the United States
57239LVS00004B/16